To All Those I've Killed Before

J.L. HYDE

First paperback edition August 2025

Cover Design by Allsweet Studios and Brandon Kobs

ISBN 979-8-9871631-6-0

(Paperback)

www.jlhyde.com

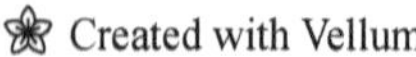 Created with Vellum

Preface

Author's Note

I've never felt the need to include a trigger warning page in one of my novels until now. Please know that this book contains several scenes of domestic violence that can (and should) be upsetting to read. I wouldn't have included them if I didn't believe they were incredibly important parts of this story.

As with all my books, there are no scenes of sexual assault; nor will there ever be scenes of child or animal death.

If you or someone you know is being abused, you can get anonymous, confidential help 24/7 by calling the National Domestic Violence Hotline at 1-800-799-7233 or 1-800-787-3224 (TTY) now.

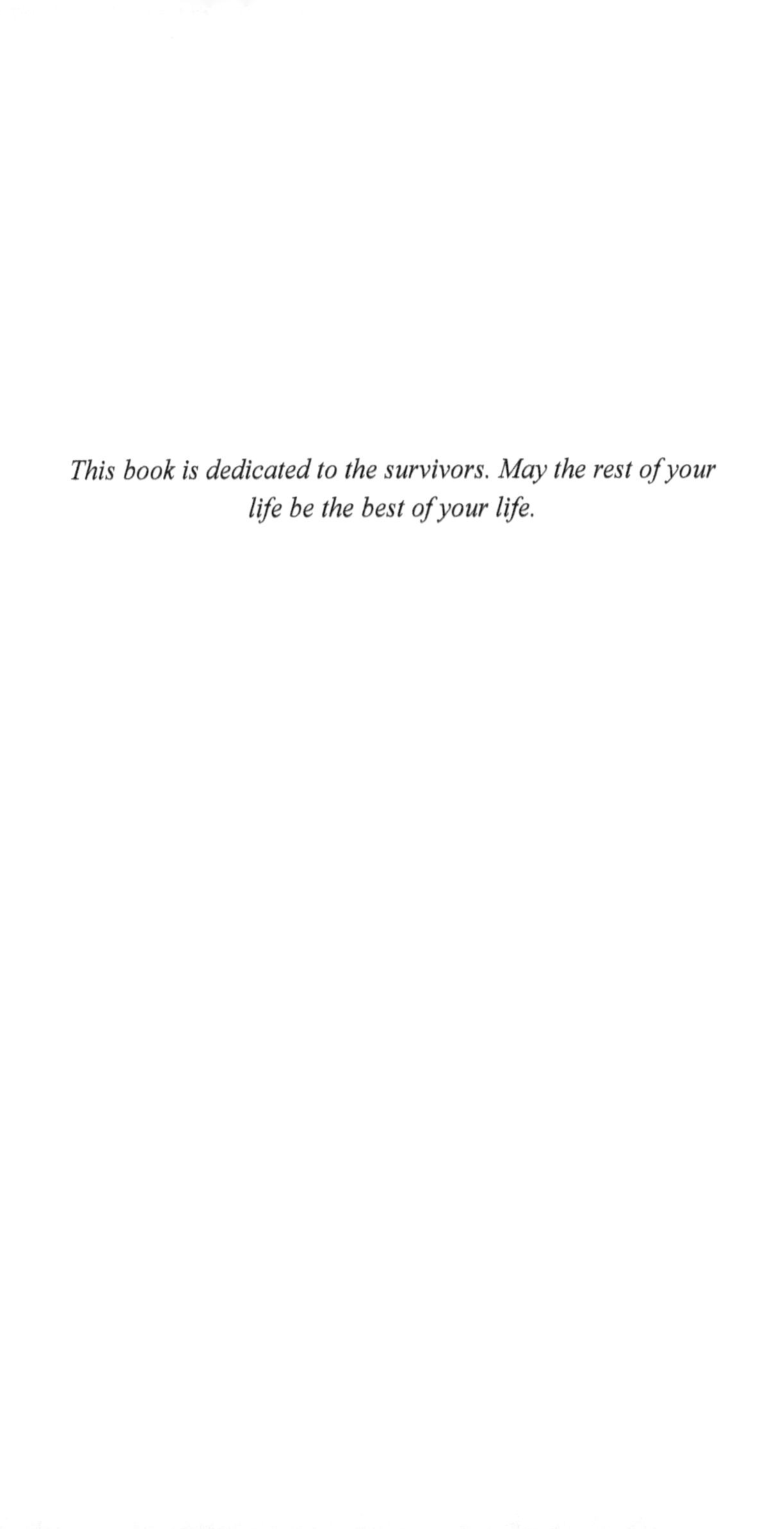

This book is dedicated to the survivors. May the rest of your life be the best of your life.

"If guys don't want me to write bad songs about them, then they shouldn't do bad things."

-Taylor Swift

Prologue

"Please explain why me dying has to affect your dinner plans," Rachel says, throwing her hands in the air. "I solemnly swear not to kick the bucket until you've finished your triple chocolate meltdown."

She quickly does the sign of the cross with her right hand as she delivers her promise, not entirely sure that it's the correct gesture but figures it can't hurt.

"How can you joke at a time like this? I thought this was the one time in your fucking life that you could manage to be serious, but you can't even give me that?" Linnea shouts before reverting to a series of heaving sobs.

"Okay, okay, let's just take a breath. Aunt Rachel didn't mean to be insensitive, I'm sure," Kim says, leaning forward to rub her daughter's back while shooting daggers at her sister out of Linnea's view.

The news came last week, and after the initial shock wore off and the acceptance creeped in, the rest of their days were spent wondering how the hell they were going to tell Linnea that her favorite aunt most likely wouldn't live to see her college graduation. Oddly enough, moving Linnea into her dorm at college was the event that inspired Rachel to book an appointment with the family doctor. Moving a few boxes up one flight of stairs shouldn't have been enough to leave the forty-one-year-old gasping for breath, let alone cause her to be bedridden and writhing in pain for days after.

Had she ignored a few earlier signs? Sure, but everyone complains about aches and pains when they turn forty—she assumed it was par for the course. She'll never forget the look in Dr. Lam's eyes when he delivered the news. Based on Rachel's reaction, which was staring blankly at the man and waiting for him to say it was all a cruel joke, he gently suggested she call someone to come pick her up so she wouldn't be behind the wheel while in such a *fragile* state of mind. She must have called Kim, but she has no memory of getting her phone out or scrolling to select her sister's name.

"You're scaring me," Kim had told her as Rachel walked out of the hospital, entered her sister's car on the passenger side, and stared straight ahead through the windshield for the entirety of the drive home, without speaking a word.

"It's cancer," Rachel whispered as they pulled in the driveway, not able to turn her head and see the reaction on her only sibling's face.

"Where?" Kim asked, her eyes frantically searching Rachel like the disease might light up, signifying the part of her body it was eating away at.

"Everywhere," Rachel responded.

Now, a week later, they've delivered the news to Linnea and she's taking it as expected, if not a little worse. Refusing to acknowledge words like *metastases* and *pericardial effusion,* and instead focusing on *terminal* and *refusing treatment*, the eighteen-year-old is inconsolable.

"This isn't fair. You can't just give up," Linnea pleads, dropping to her knees in front of the recliner where her aunt is perched.

"I know, kid. Remember what I've been telling you for years? Life can be so wonderful, but there will also be moments where it will kick your ass with no warning. It absolutely isn't fair, and that's why you have to take the moments that give you joy and hold onto them for dear life. That's the reason I'm not going through treatment. The cancer has spread everywhere, Linny. Treatment would make me very sick and just prolong the inevitable. I want to stay *me* for as long as possible."

Linnea is listening to the words but shaking her head as they come, denying them entry. Some part of her may actually understand what her aunt Rachel is telling her, but she refuses to accept it. This can't be happening. It will be like losing a limb.

"What if you just tried a little bit?"

Rachel's lips curl at the edges, but the movement doesn't reach her eyes. "Maybe just a shot of chemo to see if I like the taste?"

Linnea scoffs.

"Let's calm down on the jokes, sis," Kim says, her thumb dancing on the edge of her lighter, daring to break the no-inside-smoking rule she's had since they bought the house over a decade before.

Rachel does her best to explain the situation, sans her signature humor. "Sweetheart, if it was just breast cancer, I'd be fighting it with everything I have. But it's not. Now it's about having quality of life with the time I have left, and I can't think of a better final act than spending it with the two women I love the most and telling you both how much you mean to me, so you'll never doubt it for a minute once I'm gone."

"What about Dad?" Linnea asks, gesturing to the garage, where her father is working on his overpriced motorcycle that always seems to need fixing.

"My last breath will be spent reminding him what an asshole he is; that's a promise."

"Rachel!" Kim says, slapping her arm.

"That hurt, Kim. You probably just helped some more cancer develop with that disturbance of cells," Rachel says, rubbing her bicep. "Linny, I'll spend some time with your dad, too. I'll try to take it easy on him, but no promises."

Linnea nods, relieved that her aunt and father might stop their constant squabbling now that she's been diagnosed as terminal.

"We're going to help Aunt Rachel clear her house out in the next few months and get it ready for sale. Then we'll move her into the guest room so I can be here to help her with whatever she needs," Kim explains to her daughter.

"Your mom is going to wipe my ass and feed me pudding," Rachel adds, raising her eyebrows a few times.

Kim lifts her hand to slap her sister again but stops short. Rachel cocks her head slightly and holds up her index finger as a reminder. She wishes someone warned her as a teenager that they'd still be bickering in their forties.

"Hey, kid," Rachel begins, leaning forward and grabbing both of Linnea's hands and holding them tight, "I know you don't think it's possible, but everything is going to be okay. I've never lied to you before, and I don't plan on it now. We're going to spend so much time together in the coming months, you'll be thankful for the break when I'm six feet under."

Linnea shakes her head, knowing nothing is going to stop her aunt from joking, not even impending death.

"Can I see you every week?" Linnea asks. "I could take a semester off and see you every day. I could move back in and help mom."

"This ass only requires one person to wipe it, and there's no way I'm letting you take a semester off. You pick a day of the week, and I promise I'll clear my busy schedule to spend it with you. It will be our special day."

"Mondays and Tuesdays my course load is pretty light. I think I'm done by noon both days."

"Let's do Tuesday. It will be like our own little version of *Tuesdays with Morrie.*"

"Doesn't Morrie die at the end?"

"Yeah, but those Tuesday meetings inspired quite the story, didn't they?"

"Tuesdays it is," Linnea responds, wiping away the last of her tears. She makes a silent vow to stop crying in front of Aunt Rachel. She's going to show her how strong she can be, no matter how much her heart is breaking.

Linnea pulls both Rachel and her mother into a hug, knowing their lives will never be the same again.

One

SIX MONTHS LATER

"WATCH THIS PART," Rachel tells Kim as she sits a little straighter and accepts a wooden tray over her lap. "He just got to his new girlfriend's house for dinner and his stomach's been giving him problems all day. He's trying to tough it out and not crap his pants, and then in walks her sister and he realizes it's a girl he hooked up with a few weeks ago. Talk about a bad day."

Canned laughter from the sitcom she's watching sounds from the flat screen TV perched on top of the dresser in her room. Rachel swallows a few pills and laughs at a punchline from the show before washing them down with water.

"Who are you and what have you done with my little sister? This is the exact brand of humor you would typically mock and chastise me for laughing at. Maybe we should ask Doctor Lam to take another look at your latest scans," Kim teases. "I think the disease *has* spread to your brain after all."

Kim laughs to herself, and Rachel indulges her with a smile because it's the closest thing to a joke that her sister has managed in years. She's also indulging her by not fighting the nightly dinner service, as she did for the first month in her sister's guest room. It was her teenage niece of all people who helped her understand that cooking dinner for Rachel made Kim feel useful, like there was something in her control that she could do to help.

"Just add it to the list of things I regret—acting too cool to just enjoy things. I hate that I cared so much about what people thought of me. Well, it's better late than never, yeah?"

"All that suffering for the sake of being cool, and in the end, it didn't even work," Kim quips after securing the legs of Rachel's tray in place on either side of her thighs. "I'll be right back."

Moments later, she returns with a plate of steaming chicken pot pie and a glass of milk, carefully setting them both on the tray and pulling a napkin and fork from her back pocket and presenting them like a magician.

"Milk for dinner again . . . You know I'm not actually a nursing home patient, right? I'm still younger than you; I just have cancer."

"It's good for your bones," Kim says with a wink before standing back to assess the set up. "Anything else I can bring you?"

Kim's eyes meet hers and Rachel detects the sadness that Kim tries so hard to hide these days. The skin under her eyes is dry and darkened. She hasn't worn makeup in months, and she's developed a nervous tick of tapping her thumb and ring finger together when her hands aren't holding anything. She promised Rachel that she'd cut back on smoking, but she hasn't kept her word. Kim checks on Rachel several times throughout the night, and it's not the creaks of the heavy oak door being pushed open that wake her; it's the stench of cigarette smoke poorly masked by the bottle of Febreze Kim sprays on herself whenever she reenters the house after a middle-of-the-night smoke break.

"You should get out of the house tomorrow. Go do something for yourself—my treat," Rachel offers. "Linny will be here with me most of the afternoon, anyway. We don't need you snooping around our private conversations."

Kim scoffs before considering the offer. "Mike has a doctor's appointment in Green Bay. I suppose it wouldn't kill me to go with him and get out of the house for a few hours."

"And if it *does* kill you, I'll be shortly behind you," Rachel responds with a wink.

Something about Kim's dramatic huff each time Rachel makes a death joke brings her immeasurable joy. She'll be offending her sister until her dying breath.

"Also, how is that doing something for yourself? Why don't you get a massage while he's at the doctor? He's a big boy; he can handle an appointment by himself."

"I don't know why you're always looking to pick a fight with him," Kim says.

"Kim, he's damn near fifty years old. All I'm saying is that he should be able to handle a doctor's appointment on his own while you go and enjoy yourself for a few hours. You deserve a break. Taking care of my decrepit ass is only going to get harder in the coming months. Do something nice for yourself while you can."

Kim flinches at the mention of Rachel's condition getting worse. It's inevitable, but still hard to accept. There is no reversing course at this point in the illness, despite what Kim's high school friend Krista told her via Facebook Messenger about the miracle cure that is essential oils (and conveniently, it only works if it's the specific brand she happens to sell from her living room).

"I'll think about it," Kim offers before leaving the room.

Rachel knows she won't. Kim has been putting everyone else in her life first, long before Rachel's diagnosis. Their father used to say that his oldest daughter will die broke because if she had a hundred dollars, she'd give away ninety-nine of it without remorse. Rachel used to argue that it wasn't something to be criticized; it was admirable. Her sister is a saint. Now she understands her dad's sentiments—you can't pour from an empty cup. It's wonderful to be a generous person, but if you're giving away all your time, money, and energy, what's left for you?

Aside from genuinely wanting Kim to take some time to recharge, Rachel would also selfishly like to have the house to herself tomorrow when her niece arrives. She has spent the last few months really bonding with Linnea and giving her all the life lessons she can fit into their once-a-week meetings— the importance of saving money, being kind, working hard, and standing up for herself.

Now that her health is deteriorating, it's time to start confessing. She doesn't have much time left on this earth, and Rachel would like to depart knowing that she's confessed all of it to somebody. She'll leave this world with a clear conscience if it's the last thing she does.

"Linnea Way, reporting for Tuesdays with Auntie Rach," Linnea announces as she bumps the guest room door open with her hip, both hands wrapped around a brown paper sack. "And, I've brought reinforcements."

"Tell me that's Thai food and I'll put you back in the will," Rachel says, inhaling deeply. "Mango sticky rice?"

Linnea sets the bag down on the small table near the bed and shrugs off her coat, throwing it on the reading chair that sits a few feet away from the side of the bed. Unfolding the legs of Rachel's wooden tray with one hand, she places it over her aunt's lap in one fell swoop. Her aunt nods in appreciation as Linnea seamlessly pulls the white takeout containers from the bag and places them on the tray.

"And when did I get taken out of the will?" Linnea asks, eyebrows raised.

"When you told your mother that I was in here doing weed gummies. Nobody likes a snitch."

"I already told you—I thought she knew. You rarely leave the house—who the hell is getting them for you?"

"First of all, your mom wouldn't know a good time if it

bit her in the ass, and she certainly isn't cool with having *illegal drugs* in her house, regardless of how many times I remind her they are legal. Second, you don't need to know how I'm getting my drugs. Now hand me some napkins and get out of my way."

Linnea shakes her head and pulls the small table closer to the chair as she takes a seat and begins unpacking her own dinner.

"Do they help?" she asks.

"Who?"

"The weed gummies, Rachel. Focus."

"Oh," Rachel says, shrugging. "I suppose they do. I feel much more at peace with what's happening for a little while. I'm starting to feel really achy at night, and they numb the pain enough so I can get a full night's sleep. Oh, and they don't give you a hangover like when you have too much wine. I know you wouldn't know anything about that, since you're not twenty-one yet."

She winks at Linnea, who blushes slightly.

"It's just all so unfair," Linnea says, barely above a whisper. She flinches as a plastic spoon hits the table in front of her. Her eyes travel to Rachel, who isn't laughing.

"Linnea Jane Way. That's enough. We promised we weren't going to have that attitude anymore. We're going out with grace and acceptance, like the badass bitches we are. Now give me that spoon back; I need it for my soup."

Linnea shakes her head and stands to hand the spoon back to her aunt. "I just had so many plans for things we would do after I graduate—trips we would take, places we would see. I'm sorry, it just feels like we're getting cheated."

"And if someone you love got hit by a bus tomorrow, you'd also feel cheated, but at least with me you have the luxury of forewarning. You have months to tell me how great

I am and how stunningly beautiful I remain, despite the terminal cancer," Rachel replies, trying to lighten the mood. "Also, I'll be leaving you and your mother enough money to take all the trips. I'll even have a talk with her about trying to lighten up and have some fun, for your sake."

"Well, if I'm going to have an aunt die and leave me in the will, I guess I'm glad it's the rich one."

"As you get older, you'll realize I was never rich. I just have a few extra bucks because I chose not to have children," Rachel says, tapping her temple with her index finger.

Linnea considers this for a moment before adding, "Dad's sister, Wendy, doesn't have kids and she's still broke."

"Your dad's sister, Wendy, can't hold down a job and spends her time gambling on penny slots and sucking down wine coolers while she works her way through all the men in Alger County she isn't related to. She may not have kids, but she also doesn't have any damn sense. That's why she's broke."

Linnea gasps before losing her composure when Rachel shrugs and slurps her soup, as if she didn't just hurl the most offensive filth toward Linnea's only other living aunt. It was cruel, but Linnea can also admit that it's true. Her aunt Wendy is a mess.

They spend the remainder of their meal making small talk, with Rachel trying to distract Linnea so she'll forget what's happening and Linnea answering Rachel's questions with half-hearted answers because her mind is stuck on the sense of impending doom in the air. Both women dance around the conversations they should be having. They can spend a year's worth of Tuesdays sitting in this room and sharing meals together and it won't change the fact that in the end, she's losing her aunt. Pretending it isn't happening isn't doing anyone any favors.

Once Linnea has returned from taking the to-go containers straight to the trash bin outside—so her mother won't lecture her about stinking up the kitchen—Rachel pats the foot of the bed and invites her to sit down.

"Actually, why don't you close the door before you sit down?" Rachel asks.

"Why? Mom and Dad are in Green Bay."

"We might get caught up talking and not hear them pull in. I'd rather what I'm about to tell you stays between us."

Linnea's eyes widen slightly at the idea of having a secret with her aunt. She decides for once that she'll keep this one tight to her chest instead of running to tell her mother the minute she gets home, as she normally would.

"Is it about the will? Are you going to leave something funny to Dad? I could see you getting one last joke in on your way out."

Rachel smirks and shakes her head. "Nah, the will is pretty cut and dry. I do have some ideas for final pranks on your dad, but we can talk about those when the time gets closer. Tonight I want to show you something."

She reaches under her side of the mattress and pulls out a white standard-sized envelope. It's sealed with one of Rachel's monogrammed stickers and has Linnea's name on the front.

"When I die, and not a moment sooner, I want you to open this envelope. There is something very important I'd like you to have. Don't you even think about trying to sneak a peek when I'm not in this room or I'll know immediately. It's of no use to you unless I'm gone. Got it?"

"Got it," Linnea responds, holding three fingers up in a Girl Scout's salute. It makes Rachel smile to think about how sweet her niece was in that little uniform, selling cookies at a folding table outside the mall a decade ago. Rachel always waited until the sale was almost over so she could find out how many boxes short Linnea was of her goal and buy them all. Everyone at the office was overjoyed when Rachel would show up on Monday morning with an overflowing case of every kind of cookie on the list and hand them out for free. In school, Linnea was the one with the *cool aunt* who bought whatever she needed to from her school fundraisers so her niece could choose the biggest prize from the catalog.

"I'd like to spend the next few weeks telling you some stories that I've never told anyone," Rachel says. "There's no doubt in my mind that you're the right person to tell them to, but you need to know that they are going to be hard to hear at times. I've done some things I'm not proud of, but I think if you listen, you will understand why I did them. Most of the things I'm going to tell you happened before you were even born or when you were just a baby. It was a long time ago, but they are fresh in my mind like they happened yesterday. I've got to get these things off my chest before I die. What do you think? Can you handle it?"

"Bring it on," Linnea says with an assertive nod. "But, can we have some of this while we talk?"

She reaches forward into her oversized purse and pulls out a Walgreens bag containing a cheap bottle of red wine. Rachel smiles and chugs the last of her water before holding out her empty cup. Linnea twists off the top, gives her aunt a generous pour, and then pulls the lid off her insulated travel mug to do the same.

"I know I'm only eighteen, but—"

"Kiddo, I don't care how you got it, and I don't care that you have it. Just don't tell your buzzkill mom or she'll be mad at us both. Oh, and drink up—you're going to need it."

Three

THE FINAL DAY of middle school had finally arrived. My friends and I sure talked a big game about going to high school that fall, but the truth is we were terrified. There would be three classes of boys above us, which was enough to make us want to pass out. There would also be three classes of girls above us, which made us want to blend in with the crowds so we wouldn't be singled out. The older girls could be so mean, especially when the underclassmen did anything to draw attention to themselves.

Unseasonably warm without a cloud in the sky, we decided to ride our bikes to the beach after school. You need to understand that back then, there were no cell phones. No social media. Our parents had no idea where the hell we were, and most of them were still at work anyway. Nothing bad ever happened around here; why would they worry? We had to be home by six for dinner, and if we went back out with our friends, we had to be home for the night by the time the streetlights turned on. We may have caused a little trouble in those days, but none of us were stupid enough to stay out past curfew. Summer break was upon us; we couldn't afford to be grounded and miss out on any of the fun.

We were wild and free, kicking our legs out to the sides of our gliding bike tires after furiously pedaling for blocks. Monica put a radio in the basket of her bike and inserted a cassette tape into the deck so we could listen to "MMMBop" by Hanson on repeat while we biked to the lake.

We didn't have towels or swimsuits, and the water wouldn't be warm enough to swim even if we did, so we found a picnic table and perched ourselves on the top, staring out at Lake Michigan and talking about our plans for the best summer yet.

We weren't at that beach for ten minutes before they arrived. The four boys, just finishing their junior year and preparing to be seniors, sniffed us out like fresh meat on the grill. They knew we were coming to their turf in the fall, and they wanted to lay claim on us before their classmates even knew we existed. The tallest, most handsome of the group approached me at the foot of the picnic table.

"I'm Tyler," he said to me, reaching a hand out to shake mine like we were adults at a banker's convention. I'd never had a boy try to shake my hand before. Of course, I already knew who he was. You'd have to be living under a rock not to. Starting right wing on the varsity hockey team, son of the police chief, and youngest of four brothers—all of them beautiful, bronzed gods in this tiny lakeside town. The only question is, what could he possibly want with me?

"I'm Rachel," I answered, limply taking his hand and flinching as he squeezed mine tightly in return.

"You girls going to be freshmen?" his friend asked.

"Yeah," my friend Sophia answered, casually tucking her hair behind one ear and pretending she wasn't internally screaming.

"Nice," Tyler replied to Sophia, but never broke his eye contact with me. It made me so nervous, I had to look away. At fourteen years old I knew next to nothing about sex, but there was no mistaking the reaction my body had to the attention he was giving me. Those deep brown eyes stared directly through me, and I felt a dull throbbing in places I wasn't sure were supposed to throb at all.

"We're headed to the Dairy Flo. You guys wanna come?" the friend asked.

All four of us failed miserably at keeping our cool while responding with enthusiastic nods. Four soon-to-be seniors just invited us to hang out with them in a very public venue—the burger and ice cream shop was the busiest place in town on a sunny day. Without a doubt, we'd be seen together. The thought of heading to high school as a group of freshmen with established reputations as cool girls was almost too much to handle. We couldn't dream of a better scenario.

The ride to the Dairy Flo was less than a dozen blocks, but it could have been five miles for all we cared. We were entirely transfixed by the older boys zipping in and out of traffic on their mountain bikes and hopping up on curbs like they were auditioning for the X Games. If cars honked at them to get out of the road, the boys would stick out their tongues and wave their middle fingers in the air. These boys were *it*. The only time we took our eyes off them was to look at each other in amazement and disbelief over our luck. We were going to be the coolest freshmen in school, and September could not come soon enough.

I tried to play it cool while we stood in line to order, but I only had two dollars in my pocket, and I knew it wouldn't go far. I said I wasn't hungry and ordered a small Pepsi, but Tyler could sense my struggle from a mile away. With his wallet full of tens and twenties from working nights and weekends at the sporting goods store, he ordered two cheeseburgers and a double order of cheese fries, a subtle wink the only hint that he understood I was broke.

I'm not sure I'd ever been self-conscious while eating before that point, but I overanalyzed every chew and swallow while Tyler focused his attention on me in the back corner booth. I was certain I had something stuck in my teeth, so I ran my tongue over them frantically any time he'd look away. He and his friends weren't nervous at all; they did Adam Sandler impressions and threw crumpled up straw wrappers at each other while us girls sat and watched in wonder.

Everything they said became the funniest thing we'd ever heard. After this night, we'd quote them amongst ourselves for weeks. Remember when Tyler said "Nudie magazine day?" Oh my gosh, and remember when he pretended the fries were walrus teeth? What about when they called Mrs. Pearson by her first name and said she was a boner donor?

The eight of us spent most of that summer together. We'd meet at the beach after breakfast and not go home until dusk. If one of the boys had to work a shift at their summer jobs, we'd all ride our bikes there to harass them. If one of us had to leave for a mandatory family vacation, the rest of us would spend the week telling stories about them like they'd gone off to war. We played truth or dare and spin the bottle, which resulted in my very first kiss, followed shortly by my second, third, and fourth kisses.

I think of that summer as my sexual awakening. Everything was brand new. I learned, I lived, I loved, and by the end of the summer . . . I killed.

Four

I'M NOT sure if nobody told me, or *did* tell me and I just didn't listen, but what you feel as a fourteen-year-old most likely isn't really love at all, no matter how strongly you feel it.

The boy you dream of when you're lying on your stomach, chin perched on your knuckles and legs kicking back and forth in the air, barely resembles the boy he actually is; you're simply creating a version of him you see as perfect. It's like watching a Jonathan Taylor Thomas movie and convincing yourself he'd place his jacket over a mud puddle for you if you met in real life. But who has time for such an inconvenient truth when you're certain you're in love, right? There's a reason fourteen-year-olds can't legally consent to much of anything—our brains aren't even fully formed yet.

I should have known Tyler was no good by the way he treated his mother and sister and the way he idolized his brothers, who were all absolute menaces. I changed the narrative to suit the person I wanted him to be. This boy had me agreeing that his mom was a total bitch for making him come home early to help with chores, although I would never dream of speaking of my own mother that way. I began to agree that, although his brothers all treated women like they were objects rather than human, they were strong, masculine, small-town heroes with bright futures. They were misunderstood. Even when the oldest one joked about Tyler taking too long to "pop that freshman's cherry," he was only joking. I had no right to be scared or offended. Boys will be boys.

Believing you're in love with a seventeen-year-old boy is like being in a cult, and no, I don't care how dramatic that sounds. It's the truth. I wouldn't listen to reason, even if you spelled the facts out in perfect English. I'd have followed him anywhere. The worst ideas suddenly made sense when they came from his lips. Any other girl who spoke to him became my enemy. If he didn't call my house to say goodnight, I would stay up half the night with an intense stomachache, just staring at the caller ID and begging for it to light up with his father's name. When he'd ramble off some excuse the next morning for why he couldn't call, I'd believed every word of it.

When you're dealing with a master manipulator, even at that age, they don't hit you with the big lies all at once. Instead, they sneak in the dishonesties in small doses to check their boundaries with you. If you're a small-town girl who just finished the eighth grade, chances are you don't even understand the concept of setting a boundary yet.

All the little white lies he told me that summer are so obvious now, but at the time I ignored that feeling deep in my gut that told me I was being deceived. When the guys would joke about Tyler staying up too late because he was chatting on ICQ with the prom queen from two towns over, I laughed along. Tyler wouldn't do that to me, right?

"Do you really want to start high school as a virgin?" he asked me one late August night.

I stared deeply into his eyes after he asked the question because I wanted to see the guy I was so crazy about. The one who made me weak in the knees and desperate for his attention. But something in the way he was pushing me to do something I clearly didn't want to do made him so unattractive to me. He was the desperate one, not me.

Just the week before, I was using the public bathroom at the beach house when I heard Tyler talking to his friends in the men's room. The acoustics from the nearly empty facility amplified their voices, and it surprised me that they didn't realize how loud they were being. Or maybe they just didn't care. The guys were giving Tyler a hard time about not "sealing the deal" with me, although I knew for a fact that none of them had gone all the way with my friends. We told each other everything. Although Monica and Sophia had gone to second base, Jen hadn't so much as made out with her summer boyfriend. They were lying to Tyler to put pressure on him.

I stood quietly in the bathroom after doing my business and not flushing the toilet, for fear they would hear me and stop talking. I could hear every word as Tyler laughed about how he only had a few weeks to get in my pants so he could move on and find someone else to take to homecoming in the fall.

"This bitch is talking about going to pick out a dress, like I'd actually take a fucking freshman to homecoming," he said, while the other three laughed along with him.

This bitch.

Just the night before, Tyler talked about matching his tie to the aqua colored dress I picked out of *Seventeen* magazine and said he'd pick up extra hours at work so he could afford to take me to the nicest restaurant in town for dinner before the dance. Now he's too embarrassed to take me? As if I needed confirmation that this wasn't all a cruel prank, he continued about how they all needed to dump the freshmen before school starts so they wouldn't be wasting their senior year with "children."

"So, what if she doesn't want to fuck, man?" one of them asked.

"She weighs ninety pounds soaking wet, bro. What's she going to do?"

I had to steady myself on the wall after hearing that last line. I willed myself not to get sick because I knew it would be too loud.

I exited out the side door of the beach house and quickly ran back to the shore where my friends were lying on their blankets, listening to Usher because it had been three months, and we were no longer girls who listened to Hanson. We had tan lines, cherry lip gloss, and a firm belief that we were cooler than all the other girls in our class. And for who? Four boys who wanted to use us and move on.

Something changed in me that day. I saw myself the way Tyler was seeing me—an easy target. No self-esteem. No will power. No standards. Pathetic. A child. That's when I decided it was over between Tyler and me, but not before I left him with a parting gift.

That night in late August, I didn't plan to kill the boy who wasted my summer. I only wanted to embarrass him. To show him that I had my limits. I was half his size—how would I be able to take his life, even if I wanted to?

I almost didn't accept his offer to meet him down in the park because I didn't have to guess what his plans were for me; I'd heard them loud and clear in the boat house. I grabbed a paring knife—still in its sheath from the in-home cooking ware demonstration where my mom purchased it— from our kitchen on my way out the door and tucked it into the back waistband of my underwear. I wasn't sure I'd have the guts to actually cut him with it, but I could at least threaten him and run if things went south.

So there we sat, out past curfew because my parents were in Wisconsin for a work trip and Kim was in charge, and I weighed my options. It was all happening much sooner than I expected. Within five minutes of arriving at the playground, this son of a bitch was unbuckling his belt. He was preparing to unzip his pants after I clearly told him I wasn't ready. I frantically looked around for anyone in the vicinity, but it was a Monday night, and we were on the top platform of the playground inside the "palace treehouse," and there wasn't a soul in sight. I had my tiny pink Polaroid camera with me, under the guise of taking cute couple's photos for my locker at school. In reality, my scheme was to wait until he pulled his pants down and sneak a picture of him for blackmail. Looking back, I understand how foolish this was for a million reasons, and probably bordering on what we call "revenge porn" these days. Again, I was fourteen. Social media didn't exist yet, so I'd have to physically show everyone at school the Polaroid. That's what we considered viral in a small town, circa 1998.

He was on his knees now, inching toward me.

I can't explain the feeling, even after all these years, but it became the easiest decision to lean back and wait until he was almost on top of me. I didn't even have to think twice; there was zero hesitation on my part. His guard was down as he stopped at my feet and unzipped the rest of his shorts. I brought my knees to my chest and kicked my feet in his direction, harder than I'd ever thought possible. He didn't scream, he didn't yell, he just disappeared into the night. I heard exactly two noises—the sound of his skull cracking on a metal pole halfway down and then the sound of his body landing on the woodchips that surrounded the playground equipment.

I'm aware this makes me sound mentally unwell, but I didn't feel sorry. Not even for a second. There is no doubt in my mind that he would have lived a horrible life of using and abusing women. I stared down at his body, and when I realized it wasn't moving, I didn't shed a tear.

I climbed down from the treehouse, hopped on my bike, and even stopped for a late-night ice cream cone from the Dairy Flo on my way home. I wasn't a child anymore. I was a young woman who wouldn't be wasting another minute of her life on men like Tyler.

Five

"HOLY SHIT, Aunt Rachel. There's no way. There's no way you did that," Linnea says, wide-eyed.

Rachel doesn't say a word, only searches Linnea's eyes for confirmation that she made the right choice, that she's the one person on this earth who she could trust with this story.

"Was it investigated? Were you a suspect?"

Rachel slowly shakes her head.

"No, in fact; not at all. The department's finest put together a theory that was better than anything I could have come up with at that age. Since he had a few empty bottles of cheap liquor in his pockets—you know those tiny nips that only contain a shot—and his shorts were unzipped, they sort of pieced together this narrative that he was up there drunk and masturbating. He stumbled, fell from the edge of the platform, and was unlucky enough to hit a metal bracket for one of the pieces of playground equipment on his way down. They didn't even do an autopsy; his family wanted the case closed because any sort of investigation would mean the entire county continuing to discuss the circumstances. It was the late nineties in a small town; there may have been a few rumbles about foul play, but nothing substantial enough for them to launch an investigation over it. That fall, the county had its first tornado in one hundred years, and that became the topic of conversation for months. Tyler's unfortunate demise was quickly forgotten."

Linnea listens to every word of Rachel's explanation, her eyes transfixed on her aunt's face as she rattles off the details.

"Didn't people know you were with him? What did your friends say?"

Rachel gives her a sympathetic smirk. "Remember—we didn't have cell phones. We didn't keep track of each other's whereabouts, especially after dinnertime. I kept with the narrative that I overheard him talking badly about me and broke things off. Everyone assumed he was so upset by the breakup that he went down to the beach playground by himself to drown his sorrows. In fact, everyone seemed to feel bad for me."

"And did the day ever come where *you* felt bad?"

Rachel leans forward and puts her hand on Linnea's leg.

"Linny, this is what I'm trying to tell you. There is something deep inside me that I've worked hard to hide from everyone else my entire life. It hasn't shown its face in decades, but I'll never forget the things I've done. Now, do you see me differently? Can you continue to have these Tuesday chats with me, or do you want to stop? All I ask is that you wait until I'm gone before you tell any of this to your mom. It shouldn't be long, I promise."

As if on cue, Rachel begins to cough. Linnea can hear the phlegm dancing around in her aunt's lungs and throat as she reaches for a tissue and hacks into it. She shakes a few pills out of one of the prescription bottles next to her bed and washes it down with the drugstore wine.

"I can handle it," Linnea says. "I love you, and I just want to understand. Are you sure my mom doesn't already know? You've spent your entire lives together. You haven't even so much as hinted at the things you've done? You guys are best friends."

Rachel is shaking her head before Linnea finishes the question. "Your mom is the best person I know. I would never burden her with something like this."

Linnea laughs. "But you'll burden me? What does that say about me?"

"That I trust you. I also trust that you're mature enough to hear it and levelheaded enough to understand where I'm coming from. After I'm gone, you can choose what to do with this information. My greatest hope is that you'll help your mother understand. For now, I'm asking you to be burdened with it so I can die without baggage. Can you do that for me —you know, the aunt who has loved you every day of your life?"

Rachel bats her eyelashes and clasps her hands under her chin which, in return, inspires an eye roll from her niece.

"Of course, Aunt Rachel. Of course I can. I don't know how anything else you're going to confess to me could be worse than taking someone's life, but I'm here to listen. You've got me."

Rachel steadies her breath and squeezes Linnea's hand. This kid has no idea what she's in store for over the coming weeks. What she's about to tell Linnea will make Tyler's death seem like child's play.

They are interrupted by the sound of the garage door opening, followed by a car door slamming, a few stomps, and then the side door to the house slamming as well. Judging by the heft of the stomping coming from the hallway, it's Mike. A few seconds later, presumably after she's gathered herself, a quieter entrance is made by Kim. She gives a few light taps on the bedroom door before opening it. Her eyes are bloodshot and swollen. When she sees the looks on their faces, she blames it on seasonal allergies, which both women know is a lie.

"How did Dad's doctor appointment go?" Linnea asks.

Rachel braces herself for bad news and wonders how much more her sister can take. She can't stand Mike, but she sure doesn't want Kim to care for two dying family members simultaneously.

"We're going to have to reschedule," Kim says with a shrug.

"Reschedule? You drove all the way to Green Bay for nothing? What happened?" Rachel asks.

"The doctor was running behind because of an emergency. Mike has a lot of work to get done and couldn't afford to wait anymore. Once we were in the waiting room for thirty minutes, he decided we should head back."

"So I guess he's just going to deal with the back pain for another few months until he can get another appointment? That specialist was booked out for months," Linnea says. Rachel isn't sure if the sympathy in her eyes is for her father's pain or her mother's suffering.

"I guess so. And Rach, try not to aggravate him over this. Please. He's already in a horrible mood because of the pain," Kim pleads.

Rachel holds up three fingers in a scout's honor, just as Linnea did when she first arrived. Kim mouths "thank you" before closing the door behind her. Rachel lifts her other hand from under the covers to show Linnea her crossed fingers and cackles.

"You're a child; you know that, right?"

"A child who is dedicated to making your father even more miserable than he already is."

"I heard that," Mike yells through the door as he walks past the bedroom.

"Good," Rachel loudly responds, giving Linnea a wink. "Now, go home and get some studying done. Next week, same time?"

Six

"WELL, look who is up and around," Kim says before turning back to the stove, where she has three separate burners going. It's Friday night and, unsurprisingly, Kim and Mike don't have any plans to leave the house. Heaven forbid he take her on a date. "Want to sit out here with us tonight?"

Rachel wasn't quite anticipating the ups and downs that come with a terminal disease. She pictured the progression as a slow and steadily declining state of health, not these random, beautiful moments sprinkled in where she feels like she could jog around the block without stopping. Days like this are a cruel reminder of everything she's leaving behind in this world.

"I suppose it wouldn't kill me to eat a meal alongside my favorite people," she says, leaning forward to pinch Mike's cheek a little too hard. He brushes her hand away and returns his focus to whatever small engine part he's repairing at the kitchen table. At least he had the decency to lay a towel down under his project this time, although it appears to be one of Kim's off-white decorative hand towels from the half-bathroom.

"It'll be a race for what kills you the fastest—the cancer or Kim's cooking," he says without looking away from his screwdriver.

Kim gasps. "Michael John Way, you apologize to Rachel!"

Rachel doesn't mind it. It's nice to have some normalcy, and with her brother-in-law, normalcy means trading hateful barbs until one of them cries uncle and changes the subject.

"Relax, my dear sister. It's easy for a man who can't figure out how to boil water to make jokes about the woman who has cooked enough meals to keep him alive for over twenty years. I wouldn't have the heart to criticize the way he's tightening those lug bolts on the crankshaft of that vintage mower blade mount."

Mike sets down his screwdriver and leans back in his chair, closing his eyes as if her words physically pain him. "Rachel, none of what you just said made any damn sense whatsoever."

Rachel raises her eyebrows a few times, her lips bending into a smirk. "I took a stab, but could you imagine if I had gotten any of those words right? You would have been amazed."

Mike shakes his head and then lowers it, returning his focus to whatever it is he's actually working on, which apparently isn't a mower blade mount.

She pulls out the chair next to him and takes a seat; that's when it hits her, the lethargy that comes without warning these days. That's why she doesn't stray too far from the house when she's feeling this good—she never knows when her energy levels will crash. She fights to keep her eyes open as Kim describes in detail the recipe she found on Pinterest earlier that week and has been dying to try. Thank goodness

Kim's back is turned and Mike is ignoring her entirely because it gives her a few stolen moments to close her eyes.

Rachel jolts awake when her chin falls forward enough to hit her chest, and she instinctively grabs the table with both hands. She's not sure how long she was out, but it was long enough to have a dream about free falling off a tall suspension bridge. Kim is still talking about the loaded potato soup ingredients, and Mike is still tinkering; neither of them seem to have noticed that she dozed off. She throws in a "that's great, can't wait to try it," to which Kim turns her head slightly and smiles.

"Hey, do you remember when Mom used to make homemade chop suey for us?" Rachel asks, blinking a few times to allow her eyes to adjust to being open again.

Kim stops stirring and turns to face Rachel. "You're joking, right?"

Rachel doesn't understand how Kim could forget such a staple of their childhood; their mom made the dish at least twice a month. It was delicious.

"Rach, when Mom said it was homemade, she was being sarcastic. It was La Choy brand; it came from a can."

Rachel's mouth hangs open before replaying the memory in her head. She remembers how amazing it tasted, especially when she sprinkled those little rice noodles on top, but sure enough, she doesn't remember her sweet mother doing any chopping or dicing to prepare those meals. She can't help but laugh.

"Any other magic from our childhood you'd like to ruin while you're at it?"

Kim gazes to the ceiling to consider this before Mike interrupts. "Yeah, Rach, you were only voted homecoming queen because you gave hand jobs to half the varsity team. Sorry if you thought it was because people liked you."

"Oh, shut the fuck up, Mike. Did you know Dad's dying words were 'Please don't let my daughter marry that loser?' It's almost like he knew you'd be getting elbow grease all over the kitchen table while Kim slaves away, cooking you dinner and washing your dirty underwear for eternity."

"Elbow grease isn't a real thing, you half-wit. And I don't see you helping her with dinner, either."

Kim slaps the counter loud enough to get their attention.

"Enough, you two. *Enough*. Can we please just enjoy one dinner without you two tearing each other's heads off? I'm tired."

Rachel and Mike both shrug. Kim rolls her eyes and braces her hand on the counter so she can reach the top shelf of the cupboard for the soup bowls.

"Mike, honey, why don't you put that stuff back in the garage while Rachel grabs the saltines out of the pantry. It's time for dinner."

They spend the next thirty minutes quietly eating the soup that Kim spent hours making. She pulls up the picture on Pinterest to show them her inspiration, and Rachel must admit, her sister did a great job. It looks even better than the photos. Both Rachel and Mike nod in appreciation and act even more impressed than they actually are, for Kim's sake.

"I'm sorry, Mike. I know whatever mess you're making on the kitchen table is how you make your income, and I'll do better at keeping my mouth shut," Rachel offers.

Mike locks eyes with her, waiting for an insult to follow. When it doesn't come, he replies. "And I'm sorry for bringing up all the guys you gave handies to."

Rachel shakes her head but lets it slide; she's too tired to argue.

Kim exhales. It's not perfect, but she'll take any form of

peace and harmony between these two, so she can clean the kitchen in silence before moving onto the overflowing laundry basket. She realized a long time ago that her calling was to care for others, but damn if it isn't exhausting some days.

Seven

RACHEL HEARS her niece's car pull in the driveway and does her best to hack up everything loosely hanging in her lungs and throat so she isn't doing it in front of Linnea. There's been an alarming amount of blood on the tissues as she pulls them from her mouth the last few days, and she can't imagine how Linnea would handle that sight.

Lately she's been waiting all day to eat on Tuesdays so Linnea won't notice her lackluster appetite. If she goes long enough without sustenance, she can usually force her body into consuming whatever Linnea brings with her, giving the illusion of a healthy appetite. She knows this is yet another sign that her body is shutting down, but she's going to shield Linny from that harsh reality as long as she can. Rachel's not sure that it's the right decision, but she's a little too far gone to be considering the line between right and wrong these days. She just wants her family to be happy and oblivious for as long as possible.

She can't bear to look at the final tissue before crumpling and stuffing it into the small waste basket next to her bed. She doesn't care to know what shade of red she's coughing up tonight; it's not going to change anything.

"Tuesdays with Aunt Rach," Linnea singsongs while bumping the door open with her hip. She holds a familiar looking bag in the air and performs a quick tap dance before setting it on a table and unpacking the white Styrofoam boxes. Rachel knows it's not possible that she's carefree enough to be dancing, but damn if she isn't a convincing actress. Rachel loves her for trying.

"And you brought pasta from Antonio's, didn't you?" she asks, jutting her chin toward the picture on the bag. For decades, the locally owned Italian eatery has used the cartoon image of a plump Italian man holding a food tray with one hand and patting his rounded stomach with the other for their logo.

Linnea puts a hand under her chin, feigning innocence. "It wouldn't happen to be your favorite, would it?"

Despite the circumstances, the aroma causes Rachel's stomach to growl. She's thankful for the return of her appetite; it makes it that much easier to pretend she's feeling human tonight.

"I texted Mom; she said you'd probably want the vodka penne or the chicken parm, so I got both."

Without waiting for a response, she arranges Rachel's lap tray and places both boxes in front of her before handing over a set of plastic utensils. Linnea sits in the reading chair next to the bed and opens her own box containing an alfredo dish.

"My purse is next to you. Go ahead and reimburse yourself out of my wallet. Make sure to add a delivery and setup charge," Rachel says with a wink. When she senses Linnea begin to prepare an argument, she holds one finger up to silence her. "It's not up for discussion. Fight me on it again, and we'll be eating mac and cheese from a box next week."

"Yes, ma'am," she mutters, reaching down to retrieve a few twenties. Rachel's sure she probably isn't taking enough, which is typical. She's Kim's daughter, after all. Never looking out for herself.

"You know you're a broke college kid, right? Your face is supposed to light up when your rich aunt offers to pay for your dinner once a week. Nobody was buying my dinner at your age; that's for damn sure."

Linnea cocks her head. "I'm sure *somebody* was buying your dinner. Mom said you were pretty popular with the guys on campus."

Rachel barks out a laugh that's a little louder than intended. "When I was your age, referring to someone as *pretty popular* with the guys on campus meant they were a straight up floozy. A good time Sally. A real trollop."

"Yeah, Aunt Rach, I think that's what she meant."

Rachel gasps and yells for her sister. "Kimberly Lynn, get in this room!"

The sound of her socked feet pounding down the hallway and the subsequent whoosh of her flying through the doorway makes Rachel fight back a smile.

"What? What happened?" she asks, out of breath.

"Did you tell your daughter that I was a slut in college?"

Without missing a beat, Kim says, "I mean, you weren't spending Friday nights at the library, sis. I might have mentioned you were social in your heyday."

"She's my only niece; how dare you tarnish her image of me?"

Linnea sheepishly raises a hand. "Aunt Rach, it didn't tarnish your image. It made you seem like a badass female who was confident in her sexual identity at a young age."

Kim's lips curl into a smirk, and she motions to Linnea.

"You hear that, Rach? Being loose is empowering now. You were ahead of your time."

Rachel's eyes squint as she gives her older sister a sarcastic smile that perfectly conveys how hard she'd be popping her in the arm if she wasn't covered in takeout boxes.

"Will you leave us alone now? I'm about to tell Linny about my glory years, and I don't need your judgmental ass lurking around to hear it."

Kim shakes her head, leans forward to take a slice of garlic bread from Rachel's pasta, dips it in vodka sauce, and then turns to leave, closing the door behind her.

Eight

It was the fall of 2002, and I was young, beautiful, and full of hope that I was destined to be somebody in this world. I was living in the dorms at Central Michigan and enjoying my first taste of freedom. Not only were our parents always up our asses about what we were doing for the first eighteen years of our lives, but the entire population of our one-stop-light hometown reported back to them if they saw us hanging around. Kim and I couldn't sneeze without our parents hearing about it before we got home. It was exhausting, to say the least. Living in a world with no curfews and nobody looking over my shoulder was a dream come true.

I was matched up with a girl from my high school's rival town and two girls from the Keweenaw Peninsula in a dormitory lovingly referred to as the "virgin vault" by upperclassmen. Four girls, one bathroom; it wasn't ideal, but it was better than being home and under our parents' thumbs. By some miracle, I was passing all my classes, but I assure you that every free moment was spent going to parties, bars, tailgates, or sleeping off hangovers from the night before. My fake ID only cost me twenty dollars, and it passed the half-assed inspection by every minimum wage bouncer in town. The first time I bellied up to the sticky, weathered bar at the Wayside and ordered a Malibu Rum and pineapple juice, I thought I'd never recover from the excitement. I was an adult.

My roommate, Rainey, grew up in the next town over, but I didn't know a whole lot about her before we got matched to live together. She was a beautiful cheerleader for the team who beat us at finals two years in a row; therefore, I viewed her as nothing more than an enemy until a few weeks into our freshman year of college, when I realized she was surprisingly cool.

By October, we were inseparable. We had the same breakfast routine—bacon, egg, and cheese on a plain bagel around 10:00 a.m., watched the same shows (*Boston Public* and *Gilmore Girls*), and both had a Diet Coke addiction (ideally a fountain pop from McDonald's, which always seemed a little crisper, but our second choice was a twelve-ounce can). By some miracle, we were attracted to the exact opposite qualities in men, so we never fought over them. It sounds so silly to even refer to them as men rather than boys now, but I suppose they met the basic requirements of having a penis, pulse, and being over the age of eighteen.

I was a sucker for dark hair, tanned skin, and the thrill of the chase. Rainey preferred blonds with seashell necklaces, Abercrombie cologne, and trust funds. For the first semester, we learned to play wing woman for each other like a well-choreographed dance routine. We'd arrive at the bar, frat party, or the tailgate and zero in on our intended targets. Once we found the lucky guy who would have our attention for the rest of the evening, we would take turns mindfucking them into falling for our innocent roommate. I'd say it was like taking candy from a baby, but that would be an insult to babies everywhere because this was much easier. We had a one-hundred-percent success rate. We were good looking freshmen from a small town in the Upper Peninsula—they all assumed we were naïve and clueless, when in fact they were the ones being played. It was magic; there's no other way to describe it. Most of the time, we didn't even go home with them—it was a simple make-out session outside the bar with a little heavy petting. That's what we called second base back then—heavy petting.

Look, nobody got hurt. We weren't breaking hearts; we didn't give them enough time to fall in love. We just weren't giving them accurate phone numbers at the end of the night or making any attempt to see them again. Who knows if they would have even tried to call us, anyway? The only time I was confronted by one of my conquests on campus, I gave him some sob story about how my grandma had just passed away, and I must have given him the wrong number because I hadn't been thinking straight. I fluttered my eyelashes while apologizing and put another fake number in his contacts before ducking away into the student activity center and reminding myself to actually call my grandma, who I hadn't spoken to in weeks.

Going home for Christmas break was a drag. Mom and Dad were on my case about doing chores and even tried to impose a curfew on the nights I went out with my high school friends. The boys I grew up with suddenly seemed so close-minded and childish. Even the upperclassmen we all had crushes on failed to impress us at the local dive bar we all packed into on Christmas Eve. Moving away from our home-town had changed us. We saw the world differently.

Rainey and I counted down the days until Christmas break was over, and we could arrive back in Mount Pleasant for spring semester. I was ready to jump right back into this exciting new life we were experiencing together, but Rainey seemed a little off. She no longer wanted to go get the $2.50 burger and beer special at our favorite restaurant on Thursday afternoons and even had the nerve to opt out of Jello shot night at our favorite university bar. She spent her nights and weekends on the phone and the AOL Instant Messenger app installed on her school laptop. If I hadn't known any better, I'd have thought she met someone, but there's no way that would happen without my knowledge. We told each other everything. Shortly before Valentine's Day 2003, she confessed the truth to me over bagels at our favorite breakfast shop.

She'd reconnected with her high school boyfriend when we were home for Christmas break. At first it was casual, but it had since grown into a full-blown relationship, and she was scared to tell me. He went to Michigan State, which was about an hour away, and they were trying to make the long-distance thing work. Spoiler alert: long distance relationships rarely survive all four years of college. There's just too much temptation and too much excitement to stay interested in some lame-ass boy from your hometown when there's an entire campus of fresh possibilities.

I was confused by this development for a lot of reasons, but most of all because Rainey had countless stories about why her high school boyfriend, Brent, was a total waste of her time. He was rude, selfish, and immature. Each time we'd have another fantastic night out during the previous semester, she'd muse about how happy she was that she had broken things off with Brent before moving to Central. She said she wished she had done it years ago so he wouldn't have ruined her final two years of high school. Now, she's back with him? It just didn't make any sense.

"Rainey, are you sure this is what you want? You told me Brent was a total dick," I said, setting my bagel down and looking into her eyes for any sign of recognition. Maybe I could snap her out of whatever trance Christmas break make-up sex had put her in, and help her remember how much she was enjoying life without him.

"I knew you were going to do this. This is why I didn't want to tell you." She delivered the lines like a petulant child who wasn't getting her way. "I knew you wouldn't be supportive."

"Supportive? Rainey, you told me that he tried to control everything you did. He called your friends and pop quizzed them on the movie you watched with them the night before because he didn't believe that's where you were. He forgot your birthday during junior and senior year and was the only guy in the entire restaurant who let his date pay for dinner before prom. You said he punched a hole in the wall when he was mad at you for talking to a male teacher too long. Do I need to go on? Because I can. I've lived with you for an entire semester, and I've heard more than enough about this creep to write a damn book. You can't tell me that this is what you really want."

Rainey quickly wiped a tear away that was forming at the corner of her eye. "He's different now. College has changed him. He's sorry, and he's ready to be a better boyfriend."

I took a sip of my heavily sugared coffee drink. "Yeah, I guess we'll see about that."

"Please, Rachel. Can you at least try to give him a chance? He's really excited about meeting you."

I stared out the window next to our booth and saw the fun, careless nights I'd spent with Rainey slip away from my life. I should have known such joy could only be temporary.

Nine

I TRIED, I swear. I tried to like him. I'm a firm believer in second chances, so I put my biases aside so he could have a chance at his. I quickly realized that no man deserved a second chance less than this asshole.

He usually drove from East Lansing to spend the weekend with Rainey in our dorm, which could not have been more inconvenient. From the moment he arrived and let Rainey pay for his gas—"It's her choice if she wants to fill my tank up; I didn't ask her to!" he'd say—to the drunken snoring that kept me up all night or the empty orange juice container he'd put back in our mini fridge without replacing it, I was fed up with this clown.

I longed for the nights I used to have with Rainey. It wasn't just about the guys we had fun with; it was everything that came along with being young, wild, and free. We would laugh until we cried, we made friends with random girls in the bathroom of the bar, and most importantly, we had each other's backs. What was I supposed to do now?

I tried going out with our suitemates, the two girls from the Keweenaw in the other bedroom, but that was a disaster.

They spent over *two hours* getting ready and obsessing over their outfits, only to leave the Blackstone bar after thirty minutes because it was too crowded, and they needed to get back to the dorm to study for a chem exam on Monday. It was only Friday. They had all weekend to study. *Lame.*

My weeknights became a tired rerun of a show I no longer wished to watch: Rainey getting home from class, usually stressed because she was failing said class due to distractions by her idiot boyfriend. So, she'd try to study, and he'd interrupt with a forty-minute phone call spent harassing her about how he was certain she was cheating. She'd spend the rest of the night in tears, too sick to her stomach to eat anything with me or leave the dorms. By Friday, he'd apologize, which put her on cloud nine until the routine began again. Brent was ruining everything.

It all came to a head during our school's big rivalry basketball weekend. The campus was on lockdown, and we weren't supposed to allow guests to stay the night in our dorms, so I foolishly believed we wouldn't be graced with Brent's presence. I was wrong. She let him in through an exit door while the R.A. was busy helping one of our neighbors, who I later found out Rainey had paid ten dollars to pretend she was having a seizure. I'm still not sure how she convinced the R.A. it wasn't necessary to call a medic, but she gave the performance of her life and then shook it off, explaining she had episodes all the time and they were no big deal. Rainey and Brent tiptoed down the hall without detection.

I had been looking forward to rivalry weekend before I was even accepted into Central Michigan. The legendary weekend was even written about in *Playboy* magazine whilst discussing the nation's top party schools. Now, my roommate, the best friend I had in life at the time, would be zero fun during the biggest weekend of the year because her stupid, overprotective boyfriend insisted on coming to visit.

Physically, he wasn't even her type. He wasn't blond, he wasn't well dressed, and he certainly wasn't rich. I'm not sure what he had to offer my friend other than a shared history.

We took a taxi to the first bar of the night, which pissed Brent off because he wanted to drive his own car. I knew Rainey didn't trust him not to get behind the wheel after a few too many drinks, but she spun it as a way to avoid the inflated parking fees for the weekend, and he gave in after a relatively mild five-minute temper tantrum.

As soon as we walked into O'Kelly's bar, I spotted a guy I had made out with the previous semester. He was gorgeous, but neither one of us could remember his name after that night, so we'd lovingly referred to him as "Tongue Ring Boy." I turned around to get Rainey's attention—I knew she'd absolutely die when she saw Tongue Ring Boy was at the bar, who just so happened to be drinking with Fish Shirt Guy, a.k.a. Rainey's conquest from the same night. I did a full three-sixty after realizing Rainey and Brent were no longer behind me. It took a few seconds for my eyes to focus in the dimly lit bar and spot them in the corner, next to one of the big screen TVs. It came as no surprise to see them arguing. Five minutes into our first bar during rivalry weekend and he was already a buzzkill.

I went up to the bar, flashed my fake ID, and got three shots of Southern Comfort with lime. Maybe they just needed a drink and a breather. I didn't like the guy, but I was happy to try and solve whatever quarrel they were having so we could attempt to enjoy the weekend.

As I was walking back to their corner with my hands wrapped around three plastic shot glasses and trying to balance the lime wedges on each, I saw a group of guys standing around a pub table, wearing jerseys from our rival school. They were gorgeous, and at least three of them made direct eye contact with me, sending the good kind of chills down my spine. It broke my heart that Brent was ruining such a perfect opportunity. If he weren't in town making my friend miserable, Rainey and I would be three drinks deep with these out-of-town hotties by now, most likely choosing our favorites and making plans to go back to their hotel rooms.

I set the shots down on the table in front of Rainey and Brent, but they barely registered my arrival. The name of the tune was "I know you're cheating on me," and Brent was singing it on repeat. Doing my best to interject and calm his worries, I tapped the table, pushed the shots toward them, and looked Brent straight in the eyes.

"Brent, I know you don't know me that well yet, but my parents raised me to be an honest person. I'm telling you, from the bottom of my heart, Rainey is not cheating on you. I haven't had the luxury of a social life since you got back together, so I typically spend every night in our dorm room. You know who else is there every night with me? That's right —Rainey. Your girlfriend. Who loves you very much. Now can we just drop it and enjoy ourselves?"

"You think you're slick, don't you?"

Oh, here we go.

"Brent, you may find it appropriate to talk to your home-town high school sweetheart with disrespect, but I'm not afraid of you. You're an asshole. She may not see that tonight, but she'll come to her senses. Believe me, they always do."

Brent reached forward and took all three shots, one by one, maintaining eye contact with me between each drink. He might think I was intimidated, but I was simply annoyed. He put a hand up to cradle Rainey's face and that's when I saw it

—a bruise on her jawline. Makeup was caked on about an inch thick in an attempt to conceal it, but it was starting to rub off, and I could see the swelling and bluish tint.

"Did he hit you?" I asked, grabbing the table in front of me. "Did he fucking hit you?"

"Why don't you try something new and mind your own fucking business?" Brent barked out before taking Rainey's hand and yanking her away. She made eye contact with me one last time before they left the bar and mouthed "I'm so sorry."

* * *

My night was ruined. Rainey wouldn't answer her cell, so I sat in our dorm waiting for her to return. It was no use hunting her down at the bars in town; they were all packed for rivalry weekend, and it would have cost me a fortune in taxi fees to try. Just as I completed what I estimate to be my thousandth lap pacing around our cramped living room, the door burst open and Brent fell in, literally. The smack of his body hitting the tile was so loud, I froze in anticipation of an R.A. waking up and coming in to investigate. Rainey hurriedly closed the door and locked the deadbolt behind her.

She appeared stone cold sober and miserable. Brent, face down on the floor, attempted to push himself upright twice before slipping both times and finally giving up. He rolled over onto his back and stared at the ceiling, his eyes rolling back in his head.

He laughed when he saw me. "Bitch," he muttered before closing his eyelids shut so hard, it looked like he was deep in thought, which I'm sure was a foreign feeling for him.

"I'm so sorry, Rach," Rainey said, not making eye contact with me. "I fucked up. I ruined everything."

"Hey," I said, grabbing her by both shoulders. "No, you didn't. You're my best friend. You just had a lapse in judgement."

"What are we going to do with him?" she asked, looking down at her shit-faced boyfriend.

"How about we drag him into our room to sleep it off, and then you and I can stay out here and watch a movie? I just got the *Catch Me if You Can* DVD in from Netflix and I've been dying to watch it."

Rainey smiled and nodded. "I'll pull his arms if you can get his legs."

Slowly but surely, we dragged his inebriated ass into our bedroom, located directly off the living room. I detected a stench just before I dropped his legs onto the floor, closely followed by a growing wet stain on the crotch of his khaki cargo pants.

"Is that pee?" I gasped.

Rainey looked at me sheepishly.

"I am so, so sorry. Sometimes he does that when he gets black out drunk."

"Sometimes he just pees his pants?"

She nodded.

"Rainey, you know you've got to break up with this guy, right? He's got issues."

When I saw the desperation in her eyes, I changed my tone. "Issues we can deal with tomorrow. Let's throw on some sweatpants, and we'll have a good old-fashioned sleepover in the living room. We'll close him in here, so we don't have to deal with the smell. How does that sound?"

Instant relief washed over her. "That sounds fantastic. Thank you for being such a good friend."

We popped the movie into the DVD player, raved about how dreamy Leo has been since we first saw him in Titanic and how phenomenal Jennifer Garner's body was, and dozed off with the TV on the continuously bouncing DVD logo screen.

Shortly after the sun rose the next morning, Rainey stirred beside me. "How about I go get us some bagels?" she whispered. "We might as well be eating our favorite food when I send his ass packing. We can celebrate me being single again."

"Do you want me to go with you?" I whispered back.

She shook her head. "I need the quiet drive to clear my head and practice what I'm going to say to him."

"Good idea. Once he's gone, we could go to TJ Maxx and pick out new outfits for tonight."

"Don't you make my day," Rainey replied, that twinkle in her eye returning. I was so excited to have my friend back, I could have clapped my hands and cheered if everyone wasn't still sleeping.

She tiptoed to the bathroom, splashed some water on her face, and threw a hoodie on from a pile in the corner before grabbing her keys. "I'll be right back."

Shortly after she left, panic shot through my body. I forgot to take my birth control pill the night before. I hadn't had sex in months, but I wasn't sure what would happen if I missed a night. I remember one of the upperclassmen warning us girls to take the missed dose *the minute* we remember that we forgot it. I kept my pills in a small box in the top drawer of my nightstand, which meant I'd have to go into the urine-stench room and climb over Brent's snoring corpse to retrieve them.

I got to my feet, twisted the doorknob to the bedroom as gently as I could, and pushed it open. The odor hit me like a punch to the face. It wasn't just urine. It was vomit, body odor, stale alcohol, and God knows what else. I loved Rainey, but she was going to have to take the lead on cleaning our room because I wasn't sure I had the stomach for it.

A gurgling sound came from his mouth and nearly scared me half to death. For the first time, I took a good look at him and sucked in a breath. Urine had soaked through his pants and up through half of his shirt and dried in a small pool on the tile floor surrounding him. Vomit was all over his face, neck, chest, and also on the tile floor. His eyes were bloodshot and rolled back so high I could barely see his irises. The gurgling sound came again, and I realized he was choking on his own vomit. I remember learning in freshman orientation that one of the signs of alcohol poisoning is the lack of a gag reflex, only because it led to half the boys in class making gag reflex jokes.

My first instinct was to run to him, turn his body sideways, and help clear the airway. It only took another second for me to remember who it was lying on the ground in front of me.

So, I knelt down and I watched him choke. Thankfully, the noises grew quieter, so I didn't worry about our suitemates waking up. I watched his skin turn from pale to blue. I watched him take his last breath. I watched as his chest stopped rising and falling. I reached over his body to retrieve my pack of birth control pills, popping one of them from the foil package and swallowing it without water. I backed out of the room, closed the door, and retook my place on the discount couch we found at Big Lots before pretending to doze off.

When Rainey arrived home, I sat next to her and unwrapped my bagel sandwich. I ate most of it because I wasn't about to let the commotion of paramedics and police officers ruin breakfast from my favorite shop.

Although I didn't experience an ounce of sympathy

watching him choke to death, the thought of Rainey being the one to find him made me sick to my stomach. She didn't deserve to have that vision in her head for the rest of her life.

I went through the charade of "remembering" that I forgot to take my birth control pill, nonchalantly walking to our shared room, and slowly twisting the doorknob, as not to wake her sleeping boyfriend.

I gasped, I checked for a pulse, and then I backed out of the room and closed the door, shielding Rainey from the sight.

"Call 9-1-1," I said calmly. "Take a seat and breathe, everything is going to be okay."

She did as I said, taking a healthy four second inhale/exhale before retrieving her flip phone from the coffee table.

Though she would never admit it, I am certain she felt relieved when the paramedics arrived and announced they couldn't find a pulse. Nonetheless, they loaded him onto a stretcher and carried him to the awaiting ambulance outside the dorms.

By the time Rainey and I got dressed and drove to the hospital, a doctor was waiting for us so he could ask for the names and numbers of his next of kin.

Rainey would never have to deal with Brent again.

Ten

Linnea hasn't said a word since Rachel finished her story. Thoughts are flying through her mind, her opinion on the situation changing by the second.

Sure, this Brent guy seemed like a horrible human, but did that mean he deserved to die? On the other hand, she remembers her aunt's words when talking about Tyler, the boy she kicked off a ledge to his death in high school—he would have continued to do terrible things. Women would have suffered. Although it went against everything her mother had ever taught her, Linnea found herself applauding the decisions Rachel has made. She's always been in awe of her aunt, but learning more about the things she's done only deepens her admiration and respect.

"Was Rainey okay?" Linnea asks.

Rachel gazes through the window to her left, a robin hopping along the grass in the front yard capturing her attention. So many signs of spring are evident through this window, but she can't seem to find joy in the blooming trees or lush, green grass because she's not sure she'll be around to witness the next season's arrival.

"She was," Rachel says. "Of course, she mourned him. I think she was mourning the man she wished he was, but I supported her through it."

"Did you ever consider confessing?"

"No."

"Did you ever think about telling my mom?"

"No."

"Why not?"

Rachel inhales as deeply as her failing lungs will allow and forces a sympathetic smile. "The same reason I didn't tell her about Tyler. I didn't want to burden her. If I'm being honest, it was also probably because once I'd said these things out loud, it made them true. After going years without telling anyone, I began to wonder if they were just fever dreams. But eventually something would remind me of the fact that they really happened, and I once again would have to accept that I was responsible for it all."

"It must have been eating you alive to not have anyone to discuss it with," Linnea says, brows furrowed.

"It's why I'm telling you now, Linny. If anyone can understand and remain levelheaded while taking all this in, it's you. You're a tough cookie. And, as you've said, I've been keeping this bottled up for a very long time and I want to die without any unresolved business. That's why ghosts exist, right? They have unresolved business, so they haunt everyone and make them miserable. I don't plan on spending any time making people miserable once I'm gone; I just want to lie on a nice afterlife beach somewhere with an afterlife piña colada."

Rachel watches Linnea's eyes dance around to different spots on the comforter in front of her. She can tell she's holding something back.

"Spill it, kid."

"What do you want me to do with this information once you're gone, Rach? Do you want me to go to the police? Do you want me to keep these secrets forever?"

It pains Rachel to see the toll it's taking on Linnea. That was never her intention, although she knew it was a likely scenario.

"Do you remember the envelope I told you about?" Rachel asks, gesturing to the corner of the mattress behind her.

Linnea nods, eyes traveling to the hiding place of the mysterious letter.

"I wrote everything down for you. You won't have to wonder what my intentions are for a minute; I promise you that. You'll know what to do with this information."

Linnea's head bobs up and down with more conviction now, the relief evident in her eyes. "Okay, I can handle this. Tell me more. I want you to tell me everything."

Rachel smiles warmly at Linnea, the little girl who is now somehow an adult.

"I appreciate your enthusiasm, kid, but I'm running out of steam tonight. How about I lean back on my pillows, and you tell me about school. This semester is almost over, and you've barely told me about any of your classes . . . or your friends . . . or boys. Hell, or girls; I'm not here to judge."

Linnea moves from the foot of the bed to the reading chair next to Rachel. She kicks her feet up on the matching velvet ottoman and intertwines her fingers on her lap.

"Well, most of the guys at school are jerks, but I promise your crimes have not inspired me to let them die slow deaths; I just don't return their texts or DMs. There's this one guy I kind of like, but he's not even worthy of telling you about yet. I'll let you know if that changes."

Rachel chuckles and then winces at a burst of shooting pain coming from her right side. The pain seems to come from a new area each day. Linnea leans forward with concern, but Rachel holds a finger up and shakes her head. Leaning over to pull open the top drawer in her nightstand, she retrieves a prescription bottle, opens it, and shakes a pill into her hand. She winks at Linnea and adds a second. After ingesting them both with a drink of water, she leans back against the pillows propped up on her headboard and motions for Linnea to continue.

"You know Lyssa and Carly went to Western, so—"

Rachel interrupts her by booing loudly at the mention of her college's rival school and then holds up her hands and mouths "sorry" when Linnea shakes her head at the interruption.

"Well, I was worried because my entire senior year was spent with them. We did everything together. I don't really have any good friends to fall back on, so I was stressed the first few weeks. But my roommate, Shelly, is surprisingly cool, and her friends are nice. I'm feeling a lot better this semester. As far as classes, I don't talk about them because they all suck, and I can't wait for them to be over."

"They can't all be bad. Tell me about something interesting you've learned," Rachel says, closing her eyes.

Linnea tells her aunt about finding the lectures on ski area business management more interesting than she'd expected. She always imagined she'd move out of Michigan as soon as she got her degree, but learning the ins and outs of seasonal business management was strangely appealing to her. She talks about how she viewed the staff at Marquette Mountain in a whole new light the last time she hit the slopes. She can't imagine everything that goes into managing that beast. Just as she's in the middle of a story about costs of operation, the door to Rachel's room slowly opens and Mike peeks his head in.

He looks from his daughter to his sister-in-law and smiles when he sees that Rachel is fast asleep.

"Hey, Dad," Linnea whispers, standing to gather her things and sneak out of the room without waking Rachel.

"Hey, sweetheart. You ladies have a good evening?"

Linnea smiles. "Yeah, she just got done telling me some stories about when she was at Central and wanted to hear about my college stories, too. I guess I must have bored her," she says, pointing in Rachel's direction. She leans forward grabs a throw blanket from the end of the bed and drapes it over Rachel's chest, tucking it around her shoulders.

"I'm sure you didn't bore her, sweetie. She just doesn't have that much energy these days."

Mike puts his arm around Linnea's shoulders and leads her out of the room, closing the door behind him.

"I wasn't in any of her crazy stories, was I?"

"Why would you be in her college stories? You didn't go to Central."

"No, but I went to Mid Michigan Community College, and it was thirty minutes down the road. Trust me, your aunt always knew where the good parties were, so my friends and I spent a lot of time at Central."

"Did any of your friends date Aunt Rach?" Linnea asks, intrigued at the thought of her father and aunt hanging out with the same crowd.

"Oh, I'm not sure you'd call it dating, but a few of my friends knew her. One of my roommates hooked up with her friend for a while. She had some sort of strange name . . . Rainey; that's it. Rainey and my buddy Kyle were an item."

Linnea almost slips; she nearly asks her dad if he remembers Brent, the boyfriend of Rainey's who died her freshman year. That would mean she knew the story and that Rachel was present when he died; although it's the truth, she'd be dancing along the line of betraying Rachel's trust.

She wonders how hard she's going to have to work to keep these secrets buried deep, just as her aunt has done for all these years. She made the promise to Rachel and doesn't intend on breaking it, but Linnea is slowly realizing that keeping her mouth shut will be a lot easier said than done.

Eleven

FROM THE FRONT porch of her sister's house, Rachel sits on a white rocking chair and watches two plump squirrels chase each other around the yard, scampering up and around the trunks of every tree on the property. Crows are squawking loudly overhead, and she imagines that they are telling the squirrels to knock it off. A young couple walks by, keeping a careful eye on their young son, who is riding a few feet in front of them on his shiny new bike with training wheels. It's always a travesty when kids around here get bikes for Christmas, as the weather normally isn't nice enough to ride them until April.

"Can I get you anything?" Kim asks, peeking her head out the front door.

"Yes, you can quit worrying and come sit here with me for a minute," Rachel responds, motioning toward the empty rocking chair next to her.

"I've got another load to throw in, and then I need to marinate some chicken for dinner."

"And what happens if you put those things off for an hour? The house explodes? Armed guards come haul you away? Your face gets printed on the cover of a magazine after being voted the worst housewife of the year?"

Kim considers this. She looks back inside the house, as if someone inside will ask her what in the hell she thinks she's doing. Only, there's nobody home.

"I suppose a few minutes won't hurt anything," she says with a shrug and takes a seat next to her younger sister. "What are you thinking about out here?"

Rachel rocks back and forth a few times, taking in the sights and sounds of this beautiful April afternoon. She's not quite sure how anyone could find peace and serenity living in a place like New York City with all the concrete and chaos. Here, in the woods of northern Michigan, she knows peace; she's surrounded by it every day.

"I'm thinking about all the days in my life I should have been doing this—just sitting on a porch and watching the world go by. I've wasted so many days stressed about work, stressed about money, stressed about men. The truth is, I would have felt guilty sitting in this rocking chair, like you are now. But, why? Why do we do this to ourselves? We aren't meant to just work, and do chores, and die. We should be enjoying life. We only get the one chance at it, you know?"

Kim considers this. She scoots her chair a foot or so in the opposite direction, and Rachel knows what's coming next—the flick of her lighter. She doesn't have much time left on this earth, and she's spent enough of it lecturing her sister about smoking. She chooses to stay quiet today. Kim inhales deeply and blows a plume of smoke to her left, away from Rachel.

"I don't think men feel this way," Kim says, waving a hand in front of her face to break up the smoke. "I think it's just women who are meant to feel like we're wasting time if we aren't doing something productive."

"When I'm gone, I hope you take all the breaks you can in life. And when you're sitting in a chair, drinking a cocktail, and looking out at the water, think of me. Please, think of me and all the breaks I should have taken."

Kim switches the cigarette to her left hand and reaches over to squeeze Rachel's wrist lightly. "I think I'll be hard pressed to find a time that I'm *not* thinking of you, but that's a promise. I'll grab Linny and we'll drive to the water, mix a few drinks, and think about you."

"She's a lot like you, you know. Linnea. I'm seeing so much more of you in her as she's getting older. That terrifies me."

Kim laughs so suddenly; a cough gets stuck in her throat. "Wow, sis. Thank you so much."

"You know why it terrifies me."

"Enlighten me."

"Because we don't need another female in this family who puts everyone's needs above her own. A woman who doesn't speak up for herself and is afraid to admit what she wants in life."

For a moment, Kim doesn't say anything at all. She knows Rachel has hit the nail on the head. She can't remember the last time she put herself first. As sad as it sounds, sitting out on this porch instead of doing laundry and prepping dinner is the only example that comes to mind.

"I have a good life, Rach."

"You're an excellent wife and an even better mother. I just remember all the things that used to make you happy— sitting on the beach with a good book, casino trips, trying new restaurants, going to the movie theater. When is the last time you've done something for yourself?"

"Right now, I'm kicking my feet up on the front porch with my bratty little sister."

Rachel tuts. "I'm serious, Kim. I know it annoys you, but I keep bringing it up because it's important to me that you do things for yourself. I love you and just want you to be happy."

"I *am* happy," Kim says, but it's such a bad lie, she's not even sure *she* believes it. "Now, if you'll excuse me, I have work to do and you're just going to have to live with me doing it."

"Are you going to let me cook dinner tonight?" Rachel asks.

"Sis, you fell asleep while the roast was in the oven last week. I love you, but if letting you cook means my house might burn down, I think I'm going to have to pass. You just rest your little butt out here on the porch and tell me all about it when you come back inside."

"Do you think I'd have the strength to take care of you if the roles were reversed?" Rachel asks, not sure she's ready to hear the answer.

"No, but you have enough money to pay someone else to make sure I'm taken care of, and there's no doubt in my mind you'd spend it all for me. You're a good person, Rach. You don't give yourself nearly enough credit."

"I've done some shitty things."

"Haven't we all? I think it's time you cut yourself a break. Just try not to do anymore shitty things before you kick the bucket. Deal?"

Rachel grins. "Deal."

Shortly after Kim enters the house, Rachel remembering the name of the app from that morning's episode of the *Today Show* and downloads it to identify the birds singing around her. She smiles as she holds it in the air to record the bird song, and in less than ten seconds, the app has named three different species—song sparrow, American robin, and chipping sparrow. Maybe in another life she'll be a birdwatcher; she suddenly understands the appeal.

Her tranquility is disrupted by the increasingly loud sound of Mike's roaring motorcycle as he approaches the house, traveling down their usually quiet side street.

After pulling in the driveway, he kills the engine, removes his helmet, and hops off the bike, raising his arms in the air to stretch. He hasn't noticed Rachel on the porch.

"I thought Kim packed your bitchass a lunch today. I didn't expect to see you home this early."

He jumps slightly at the sound of her voice and then plays it off, like he knew she was there.

"And miss seeing my favorite sister-in-law?"

He winks before walking into the garage, and Rachel's pulse quickens. She's already told Linnea so much about the horrible things she's done in her life, but she shudders when she thinks of the things she hasn't yet told her. Her worst mistakes. The ones that keep her up at night while begging the universe for forgiveness.

Twelve

"THAT's the problem with you kids—" Rachel stops mid-sentence.

"What? What's the problem with us kids?" Linnea asks, skipping through songs on her Spotify app until she lands on a familiar intro from her favorite Michigan-based band, Greta Van Fleet.

"I can't believe I just said that. I'm a crotchety old woman. When did that happen?"

Linnea smiles. "I mean, you've always been my cool, rich aunt, but you've had some crotchety tendencies for a while now."

"Ouch," Rachel says, holding a hand to her wounded heart.

"You can still voice your complaint to me. I'll be sure to pass it on to my fellow youth," Linnea says, biting her cheek to avoid laughing.

"Well, we used to buy what was called a CD. That stands for compact disc."

Linnea rolls her eyes. Her mother has plenty of CDs in a case in the basement. She's not quite sure how to play them or what equipment would even be required to do so, but she's familiar with the concept.

"We would get in our cars, drive to the mall, buy the newest CD, and struggle to remove all the ridiculous plastic from the outside so we could pry the case open. We'd listen to every single song before deciding what our favorites were. Now you kids just have some app to suggest songs to you, you skip half of them, and never get to experience an album the way it was intended. When the artist recorded that album, they planned it from the beginning to the end. They wanted you to *feel* something. Listening to an entire record should be an emotional journey. We'd clear an entire afternoon to listen to one for the first time."

"Okay, Aunt Rach. Let's listen to one from when you were my age. We will lie on our backs in this bed and stare at the ceiling while we listen to every single word. We could even install a landline and prank call boys if you'd like."

"Is this a joke? My heart is weak and can't stand this kind of trickery."

"I swear. I don't have anywhere to be. Let's do it."

Rachel claps her hands together and leaps to her feet faster than she has in weeks. In fact, she's not sure she's felt this sort of excitement in *months*. She holds up a finger and instructs Linnea to wait while she quickly descends the steps to the basement and opens the door to find Kim's CD case. The quick descent takes a toll on her when the pain reaches her lungs, but she powers through. This is a monumental occasion.

She prays her sister had the good sense to keep the record that shaped their teenage years. She yelps with glee when she spots it in the first row. She unplugs Kim's radio/CD player combo from the wall next to the raggedy old pool table that nobody seems to use anymore and takes the stairs back up two at a time, her chest heaving from the exertion. There's no time to waste when preparing to show her only niece one of the most important soundtracks to her early life.

"Okay, if you need drinks or snacks, get them now. This album is fifty-seven minutes of pure genius, and you aren't leaving this room until we're done."

The very essence of being an eighteen-year-old is to pretend you're too cool to get satisfaction from spending any significant amount of time with your older relatives, but Linnea cannot help but clap her hands together and fluff a few pillows on the bed to prepare for their listening session. She reaches in her bag to retrieve a box of Reese's Pieces and offers a handful to Rachel, who gladly accepts them before pressing play and falling back onto the bed.

For nearly an hour, they listen to every single song on *Jagged Little Pill* in order, as Alanis and God intended. Linnea feels her first real dose of angst during "You Oughta Know." They tear up for no apparent reason while listening to the gentle lyrics of "Head Over Feet." "Ironic" is the only song Linnea feels like she's heard before.

When the last track ends, Rachel sits up straight and looks back at Linnea, who is still lying flat on her back.

"How old were you when this came out?"

"Look, I'm not going to lie to you, kid. I was eleven. We knew every word to every track, but didn't begin to understand the meaning until we were teenagers. By college, we understood the heartache and the nuance. Shortly after college, we learned the most devastating news about this album that you could imagine."

"Oh, no," Linnea says. "Is Alanis a bad person? Did she get cancelled?"

Rachel scoffs. "No, she's a saint. She's Canadian. We worshipped her."

"Well, then what happened?"

"We, a nation of young women, found out that this album was written about the man who broke her heart . . . and that man was Dave Fucking Coulier. Yes, that's right. Uncle Joey Gladstone from *Full House*. Can you imagine how we all felt? It was a shot directly through the heart, Linny. These beautiful words were written for the dipshit goofball who said 'cut—it—out' on Friday nights, broadcast on every TV in America. I'm still not sure I've recovered from that news."

Linnea props herself up on her elbows and stares at Rachel. "You need help."

"*You* need help if you don't understand how tragic it was."

"I'll admit, it was a good album. Next week, can I pick one that we listen to?"

"Does your little app allow you to listen to entire albums?"

Linnea nods. "I'll be back next Tuesday, Rach. You might be dying, but it's not too late to have a new favorite album."

Rachel smiles. Days like this are what she'll miss the most.

Thirteen

SUMMER IS ARRIVING in slow bursts, peeking its head in with seventy-degree days, only to be pushed back out with windy, overcast, chilly afternoons to remind everyone that the season is not officially here until the third week in June.

Linnea is on her way over for their weekly meeting, so Rachel is standing in her bathroom and applying concealer under her eyes to appear a touch more awake and alert. She's not sure why she continues to work so hard to fool her niece into thinking anything other than the truth, which is that she's most likely going to die sometime in the next few months. If she had a therapist, they'd be making a fortune trying to make sense of the things she's willing to do to avoid these conversations with Linnea. She vividly remembers the day her niece was born. She held her in her arms and silently vowed that she'd do anything to protect her from pain. Eighteen years later, she's the one breaking her heart.

Kim and Mike are in Wisconsin today, looking at yet another "project bike" for him to purchase and sink time and money into, instead of fixing the endless list of things around the house that have been broken for years or, heaven forbid, take his family on a vacation. Kim might not have detected it in his tone, but it was obvious to Rachel that he was lukewarm on the idea of her even riding along with him today. She can't imagine choosing someone to spend the rest of her life with, reciting vows in front of a crowd, only to decide that you'd rather do anything on earth than spend time with them. Every time she thinks about it, she gets irritated with him.

A car door slams shut in the driveway, and Rachel hurries her makeup application and stows her tube of concealer in the bathroom drawer. She barely has her undereye blended when footsteps sound down the hall, approaching her door.

"I've been thinking," Linnea announces when she enters Rachel's room, two salad containers in her hand. She's been noticeably veering more toward healthy meals as of late, no doubt in a bid to prolong the inevitable. Rachel doesn't have the heart to tell her that no amount of leafy greens and hearty vegetables is going to change the outcome at this point in the process.

"Thinking? You're much too pretty for that."

"I'm serious, Rach. I've been thinking about the stories you told me last month. About Tyler and Brent. Neither of those events are your fault. These aren't stories you should feel the need to confess on your deathbed. Tyler was horrible and you were protecting yourself. Brent sounds like he was just as bad, and if he didn't drink himself to death that weekend, don't you think it would have happened soon anyway? You just happened to be the unfortunate witness. I don't think either of those stories are going to land you in the bad place when you die, you know?"

Rachel stands in the bathroom doorway and watches as Linnea unpacks their salads, divvies up the silverware, and sets up her dinner tray with a packet of dressing on the side.

She really is so much like Kim in the way she cares for those around her. She's probably been overthinking these confessions for weeks, since the minute the words came out of Rachel's mouth. She's likely been mentally reviewing every detail and finding a way to look at the situation in a manner that concludes Rachel has done nothing wrong. Although it's a nice outcome, she knows her niece's judgement is clouded by her love for her. She also wonders how strong that love is, because she hasn't begun to confess the worst of it.

"That's really kind of you to say, Linny. I hope you're not going back to your dorm and worrying yourself sick over this; that wasn't my intention."

"I'm not, Rach. I just want you to know that I get why you did the things you did. If I were in your position, I hope I'd have the strength to do the same."

Rachel sits on the bed and Linnea lifts the tray over her legs. She stands back, just as her mother does, and scans the scene to see if she might be missing something. Satisfied, she takes her seat on the reading chair, pulling a foldable wooden TV tray in front of her. Kim bought it last month, to make it a little easier for the women to enjoy their Tuesday dinners together.

"Thank you, Linny. That really means a lot. I've got a funny feeling you'd have more than enough strength to do the same. Now, when is move-out day? Next week?"

"Yes, next Friday," Linnea says with raised eyebrows and a spark in her eyes. "Which means I'll be moving into the basement for the summer, and we don't have to have Tuesdays with Rach anymore, because I can see you every day."

"You know you can have this room, and I'll move to the basement," Rachel offers.

"And you know this hasn't been my room since I was twelve. Dad framed that bedroom downstairs for me the minute I became a teenager. So, no, I don't want this room back."

"Also, you will *not* be seeing me every day. You are going to be young and have a life. We'll keep our once-a-week meetings. You're about to be nineteen years old; you need to enjoy your summers before they're consumed with a thankless, soulless, miserable job in corporate America."

"Gee, I can't wait to be a real adult," Linnea jokes.

"Maybe you'll get lucky and find someone old and rich so you can be one of those girls who lives on a boat and posts on Instagram all day until he dies and you get all the money," Rachel suggests.

"One can dream, Aunt Rach. One can dream."

"Speaking of dreams," Rachel says as a segue. "You know how most dreams are either lost by the time you wake up or are so fleeting, you only remember bits and pieces, yet other dreams are so incredibly vivid, you wake up remembering every second?"

Linnea nods. "Of course. Why do you think that is?"

"I'm not sure, but the same can be said for people you meet. Some of them are forgotten the minute they are out of your sight, yet others tend to stick with you, in the back of your mind for life. I want to tell you a story about someone I can't seem to forget, no matter how hard I try."

Fourteen

IT WAS 2006 AND, against all odds, I was on track to graduate in one week. I sure as hell wasn't ready for the real world, but I gaslit myself into thinking I was so that I wouldn't have a full-blown meltdown.

Eight semesters of college flew by faster than I ever imagined they could. It felt like just yesterday I was at home with my parents and my sister, living the good life as the youngest child. Now I was expected to decide where I wanted to live, apply for jobs, and look for an apartment on my own. I heard one of my classmates complaining about how much she had to "put down" on the apartment she found, and I made a mental note to ask Dad what that even meant. Don't even get me started on health insurance and co-pays; clueless was an understatement.

During my final semester at Central, I made a new friend named April who was in my program. We had two classes together and sat next to each other in both. She was from Pennsylvania and, after knowing each other for a month or so, she began to tell me a little about her upbringing. We'd grab coffee together after class sometimes and, with the way we hit it off, my only regret was that we hadn't met sooner. We both talked about our lives back home, and it was evident she didn't have as easy of a childhood as my sister and me. She was an only child when her parents got divorced, and then both remarried and had more children. She split time between both houses, but neither felt like home to her. Her parents were distracted by their new spouses and new babies and rarely paid her any attention. She said she felt like the old toy that gets brushed aside when you get a shiny new one for Christmas. The guilt was so heavy, I nearly wept. My life wasn't perfect, but I never had a shortage of attention and love. There's no doubt I took it for granted.

April spoke with a stutter and had some sort of tick, where her head would jerk to the side, jaw would clench shut, and her hands would squeeze into fists a few times before she took a deep breath and the symptoms would normally subside. She never volunteered any explanation for it, and I never asked, mostly because I didn't feel it was any of my business, and if she wanted to talk about it, she would. To the best of my knowledge, it didn't affect her ability to learn whatsoever. She had higher grades than me in both classes, and the professors often used her research papers as examples for the rest of us to follow going forward.

College wasn't like elementary or middle school; there weren't schoolyard bullies waiting for her on the playground so they could make fun of her physical differences. Most people didn't seem to notice and, if they did, they didn't care. There were several other girls like me who befriended April and patiently waited for her episodes to end if she was in the middle of speaking when they began. You could sense that she was often interrupted or rushed, most likely by her parents, as she always seemed especially grateful for our non-reaction to her differences.

I've always been blessed with an excellent intuition when it comes to recognizing those people in life who are simply *good* to their core, and April was one of them. She hadn't been dealt the best hand in life, but she never let it get her down. She was kind, fun, smart, and ambitious. She was everything I look for in a friend. If I was having an off day and feeling low, she's the one who came through with some sort of optimistic Hallmark-card-worthy quote that would remind me how lucky I was. After speaking to her, I felt like no issue was big enough to ruin my day.

The first problem due to her disabilities that I witnessed occurred when we began rehearsals for our program's graduation festivities. The problem's name was Marcus.

Sitting in metal folding chairs in one of Central's smaller auditoriums, the unseasonably warm temps had us all fanning ourselves with the printouts we were handed upon arrival. We had to stay still while the head of our program made rounds, standing in front of each of us while he read our names and degree out loud, so we could verify that he was pronouncing them correctly. April had a unique last name, and he absolutely butchered it. She smiled politely and began to sound it out for him, and she even recited a cute little rhyme she'd always used for her teachers back home to remember, and then her jaw started to twitch, and the stutter began.

First, I was annoyed because the man appeared a little impatient. I wanted to shake him and ask how an extra thirty seconds of showing this young woman grace was honestly enough to make him act like an asshole. That annoyance was quickly overshadowed by Marcus, a student one row behind us, when he began mocking April and mimicking her stutter.

I swung my head around so fast Marcus flinched, thinking I was going to slap him. I probably should have, but the department head was still in front of us, and I needed to graduate on time. I shot him a look and hoped he could read the message behind the fury in my gaze, which was "Shut the fuck up before I knock you into next Tuesday."

Within seconds, April calmed herself enough to finish her sentence, and the man made a note on his card about the pronunciation. I reached my hand up behind April to quickly pat her back in a friendly, consoling manner to let her know I'm here and I'm sorry. She gave me a tight smile and mouthed "thank you" before we were once again cut off by the idiot behind us.

"Fucking fantastic, she's not only mentally challenged (he used a more offensive word that I refuse to say aloud), but she's a lesbian, too."

He elbowed the kid next to him, who gave an agreeable snicker in return.

"What the fuck is your problem?" I said, keeping my voice as low as my fury would allow. "Is this grade school? We're adults, you asshole."

"I just can't believe they're giving her a degree. Are the standards here really that low? This isn't the Special Olympics."

"Well, they accepted you, didn't they?" I asked, staring him straight in his cold, dead eyes without blinking.

"Whoa, are you her caretaker or something? Is this some sort of charity project?"

In that moment, April reached up and grabbed my fore-arm, pleading with her eyes for me to just let it go. This poor girl had most likely been dealing with jerks like Marcus her entire life. This wasn't new to her. I, on the other hand, was from a very small town where we didn't verbally assault our classmates, or our parents would be getting a call that very night. Nobody was anonymous, nobody could behave like a menace without consequences in a community that small.

I spent the rest of the rehearsal in silence, listening to him yap to his stupid friends about what April must be like in bed, complete with mock stuttering and raucous laughter. I was so angry, I thought I was going to pass out. My heart was beating rapidly and the rage inside me was something I didn't recognize. I wanted to tear him limb from limb. When we were dismissed, Marcus and his friends followed behind us, but his taunting of April faded into a breakdown of their idiotic weekend plans, which included making Jello shots and tubing down the Chippewa River on Friday afternoon.

As we neared the parking lot, I hugged April so hard she yelped in pain, and I had to pull back and apologize. The fury I kept bottled inside escaped me in the form of hot tears, but April wasn't crying. I think that's what upset me the most. She was used to it.

I knocked on Rainey's bedroom door the minute I got back to our apartment.

"It's our last weekend in Mount Pleasant; what's the plan?"

"Uh oh, what do you have in mind? That's a devious smile."

"It's going to be beautiful on Friday. Let's tube the Chip, one last time."

Fifteen

I HAD A PLAN A, B, and C, for how I was going to get Marcus alone sometime during the journey down the Chippewa River, but it turns out I didn't need any of them.

The second we picked out our tubes and lined up at the entry point, Rainey shot me the most pitiful, apologetic smile as she motioned toward the tall, muscular junior she hooked up with the weekend before. "Go ahead," I encouraged her. "I'm just here to vibe anyway. I'll catch up with you at the end and we'll get food."

"You are the best, Rach. Have I ever told you that?" she squealed, clapping her hands together and leaping forward to hug me. I wondered if she'd still feel that way knowing I watched her ex-boyfriend die slowly on the floor of our dorm freshman year.

I smiled as she skipped away toward last week's hookup, positively glowing as he picked her up and spun her around, kissing the top of her head. *I did her a favor*, I reminded myself, shaking my head to rid myself of the vision of Brent choking on his own vomit three years prior. It felt like a lifetime ago.

I spotted Marcus with his friends, shot-gunning cheap beer and crushing the cans on their foreheads before discarding them near a group of trees next to the river's edge. An employee from the river tubing company shook his head and collected all the groups' garbage in his hands, dumping it into a bin less than two feet from Marcus's group, not that they noticed.

The thing about most college boys is that they are simple creatures—food, alcohol, sex. That's what they want, and not necessarily in that order. As the river guide was giving his obligatory lecture about safety protocols, I made my way to the edge of the water, directly in front of Marcus, and slowly removed my tank top. I took my time adjusting my bikini top, as though I didn't know that manhandling my own chest had his entire group transfixed. I pulled a flask out of the back pocket of my cut-off jeans and pretended to take a swig.

"Ahh, she's not messing around," one of his friends said.

I shrugged with an innocent smile and said, "It's our last weekend in college. We've gotta get a little crazy, right?" I locked eyes with Marcus and winked.

"Damn right, we do," Marcus said, not hiding the fact that his eyes had undressed me about a dozen times in the last two minutes. He didn't acknowledge our conflict from days earlier at the rehearsal. Zero apologies or mention of April. He either didn't recognize me, didn't understand what an out-of-line asshole he was, or both. I wasn't sure which option was worse.

Despite the unseasonably warm temperatures, the river was still ice cold, causing me to yelp in surprise when I dipped my toes in. Marcus made a joke about me being a pussy, and I threw my head back in laughter. It was in that moment I wondered what was going to be a bigger challenge

—killing Marcus or pretending to laugh at his jokes all afternoon.

Once we were on the river, it was easy to isolate him from the group. I told him I wanted to be at the tail end because it's the best view if you want to watch everyone else get progressively drunker and fall off their tubes. The later in the afternoon, the lower the inhibitions. I don't think I'd ever tubed the Chip and not witnessed at least a few people hooking up, passed out on tubes, or pulled off to the side of the river so they could puke in the bushes. We don't get many warm months in Michigan, so when it's eighty degrees and sunny this early in the season, nobody wears enough sunscreen or drinks enough water. We just enjoy the sunshine and throw 'em back until we can't drink anymore. Sunburns and hangovers were a tomorrow problem.

I put my feet on Marcus's tube so they'd quit dipping in the frigid water, my freshly painted pink toenails purposely touching his upper thigh. He couldn't take his eyes off me. I took another false sip from my flask and then offered it to him. He gladly accepted and greedily drank from it, without handing it back to me. A selfish asshole—no surprise there. Everything was going according to plan.

I smiled lovingly at him while silently plotting his demise. He just kept drinking. This was going to be easier than I thought. Between pulls off the flask, he bored me with details of how much money he was going to be making at his uncle's firm after graduation. He was going to start there after he took a month off to explore Europe, where they have the "really good weed and hot fucking chicks." I'm sure he was the type of idiot American that Europeans just love to see getting piss drunk and littering on the streets of their beautiful cities.

I would nod and smile and throw in a laugh every few

minutes for good measure. I exaggerated my manufactured giggles, pushing my bouncing chest in his direction over and over again. He couldn't look away if he tried.

I knew from experience that a big bend in the river was coming up in the next ten or so minutes, and I watched his mannerisms, hoping he'd drank enough by the time we got there. I squinted my eyes, taking in the trees and rocks around me, trying to recognize the signs that the turn was coming. When I was certain it was near, I pulled his tube closer to mine with my legs and looped my arm through his. He raised his eyebrows a few times and licked his lips, which nearly made me throw up in my mouth. I reached forward to feel the flask on his lap, which still had an ounce or two of liquid in it.

"Drink up, pussy," I teased him. That's college boy kryptonite; don't you dare make them feel like they aren't drinking enough.

"Wow," he replied, holding the vowel sound a little too long. He downed the rest of it. I could tell by the struggle to keep his head upright that it was hitting him. I smiled. I could see his eyes beginning to lose focus as he tried to keep them on me. He looked confused. His head bobbed forward a few times before his eyes closed and he slumped to the side, leaning on me.

I put a foot down through the hole of my tube and skimmed the bottom of the river, slowing us down. My adrenaline was pumping so much, I don't think I even registered the cold water or jagged rocks when my toe hit them. I had a very small window to pull this off. I glanced at the group in front of us. They were all in their own world—drunk, happy, oblivious. Someone had a radio strapped to their tube, blasting old school rap at full volume, and half the guys in the group were shouting what they thought were the lyrics. None of them were looking back at us. I slowed us for another few seconds, just to be sure.

"Marcus," I said, shaking him. "Marcus, wake up."

He was out cold. Zero reaction. I lifted his arm and let go. It slapped down on the tube like dead weight. The view on both sides of the river was nothing but dense forest. I looked behind us. Nothing. Grabbing the flask from his lap, I dunked it in the water a few times to rinse out any remaining liquid. Next, I rotated his tube so that he was leaning away from me and with one heave, I flipped him over into the river. He didn't react. His limp body simply floated face down without a fight.

I kicked my leg off a large rock under the water, propelling myself toward the rest of the group. Catching the current, I pushed myself along as quickly as possible. Once I made the bend, I could see the group again; well, the backs of their heads. None of them turned around. I kept pushing. Within minutes, I was mere feet behind the last few tubers which, thankfully, were not Marcus's friends. It was a group of three couples, all of them bordering on too drunk to function.

"Hey," they said in drunken unison as I paddled past them. By then, I was sitting with my butt on the tube and pushing myself forward with my hands. They held their drinks up in the air to toast me and then frowned when they realized I didn't have one.

"I know, I just drank my last Coors, so I'm trying to find my roommate to get another one," I said, shrugging.

"That's a party foul!" a dirty blond, slightly pudgy frat bro yelled while holding up an enthusiastic thumbs down and making a fart noise with his lips.

"We can fix that," a sweet brunette says to me. She had a small floating cooler attached to her tube. She reached inside and retrieved a Milwaukee's Best, tossing the can underhand to me.

"Good looking out," I tell her with a wink.

I cracked open that ice cold beer, took a drink, and paddled with one hand past all the inebriated co-eds until I reached Rainey and her flavor of the week.

"There she is!" Rainey shouted, and I realized she was hammered, which was perfect. "Where have you been?"

"I made friends with a few couples back there. They were giving me beers so I couldn't leave."

"What's better than free beers?" she said, followed by a hiccup.

"Not much, Rainey. Not much at all."

Sixteen

"No fucking way," Linnea says, searching Rachel's eyes for any hint of deception. "No way."

Rachel takes a sip from the liquid meal replacement Kim is forcing her to consume this week. "I warned you that I've done some questionable things, Linny. This is the whole point of these confessions."

"What was in the flask?" Linnea asks.

"Don't worry about it. I don't need to be giving you any ideas."

"Did his friends notice he was missing right away? Did you get questioned?"

Rachel laughs in response, and Linnea is shocked by the coldness of it. She's not seen this side of her aunt before today.

"None of them noticed when he didn't pile into the van with the rest of us to be brought back to the parking lot where we started. Luckily, I was okay to drive because I only had the one beer, but his friends called a taxi. I kept waiting for them to notice he wasn't there, but they didn't. I think those guys were so used to being drunk and having members of their group wander off, they didn't think twice. I'm sure the assumption was that Marcus was off hooking up with some random chick he met, maybe even me. His body was found the next day by a fisherman, and the campus mourned another student who succumbed to the consequences of binge drinking."

"Holy shit. So, you were basically a vigilante at this point. What about April? What did she say? Did she suspect you had something to do with it?"

Rachel pauses, recollecting the details.

"You know, I don't think she even mentioned it at graduation the next day. I'm not sure she had heard the news yet, and I wasn't going to bring it up. That's the mistake a lot of people make when they're guilty; they bring it up in conversation unnaturally, which brings attention to themselves. I'd watched enough detective shows to not make that mistake. I kept my mouth shut. What I do remember is that she had a lovely graduation day, earned her degree with honors, and from what I've seen on social media, she has a beautiful life. I think about her often."

Linnea is overcome with conflicting thoughts. The first two deaths that her aunt "confessed" to were very easy to justify, and one wasn't even at her own hands. But Marcus? That was murder. It was even planned, and from what Linnea recalls from watching true crime shows, she thinks that means it would qualify as first-degree homicide. She cannot believe she's staring at a woman who *murdered* someone. Her own flesh and blood. Her mother has always taught her to do the right thing, and she knows that turning Rachel in so that Marcus's family could have closure and justice would technically be the right thing, but what would the courts even do? Rachel doesn't have much time left, judging by her newly gaunt cheeks and the increasing frequency of hacking, intense coughs. How would Linnea feel knowing her aunt took her final breaths alone in a prison cell? Horrible. That's how she'd feel. Simply horrible.

"This is surreal." That's all Linnea can come up with.

"If this is too much for you, kid, just say the word, and I'll figure out another way to get these sins off my conscience."

"No, I'll be fine. I guess I just expected all your confessions to be the same—things that weren't really your fault. Or things that could be easily excused. But you straight up drowned a man for insulting your friend, Rach."

Something in Rachel's eyes changes the minute the words are out of Linnea's mouth. Something new. A darkness.

"He didn't just insult my friend. He mocked and humiliated someone from a marginalized community. He mimicked having sex with her to his friends. He was a horrible human. It would have gotten worse."

"Look, I promised to listen while you confessed your sins, but I never said I'd stay quiet and not tell you what I thought about them. I'm not a priest. I think it's messed up what you did. I still love you. Somehow, I still believe you're one of the best people I know. My entire life you've told me to stand up for myself and do what's right. I guess I just didn't know the extremes you'd taken to stick to that philosophy."

Rachel gets to her feet and walks to the en suite bathroom, steadying herself by running a hand along the bed next to her.

"I don't know what to tell you, Linny. I can only promise you that everything I've done was with the best of intentions."

She closes the bathroom door behind her, and Linnea can hear her shaking pills from one of the prescription bottles she keeps on the sink, followed by the sound of her pouring a glass of tap water to wash it down.

She knows she only has a minute or two before her aunt finishes her business and comes back in the room, so Linnea acts before thinking it through. Rising from the reading chair, she sticks her hand under the corner of the mattress, where Rachel is supposedly keeping something important for Linnea to retrieve after she passes. She feels around and pulls two envelopes out, both standard size. She curses when she sees that they are both completely sealed, with no way of peeking inside at the contents. They feel like letters, one envelope slightly thicker than the other. She turns them around.

The first and thickest one simply says, "For Linnea."

The second is labeled MICHIGAN STATE POLICE.

Holy shit, Linnea thinks. *It's not just me she's confessing to.* Once she's gone, the police will know what she's done, too. There will be no going back once Linnea delivers the confession letter to the Michigan State Police. Will she have the strength to deliver that confession letter, knowing the world will never look at her family the same once the news breaks that her aunt was a stone-cold killer?

Seventeen

Dr. Lam has been in Rachel's room with the door closed for nearly an hour. Kim, Mike, and Linnea are at the dining room table, doing their best impression of a family who is eating a lunch of sandwiches and chips and most certainly not worried sick about what the doctor is going to say when he emerges.

"I'll be in the garage," Mike says, pushing his chair out and shoving the remainder of his turkey and Swiss on rye in his mouth. After seeing the reaction from his wife and daughter, he adds, "What can I do in here? Just fill me in after he's done. I've got work to do."

Linnea wants to believe that her dad has been so callous about Rachel's diagnosis because he's just not great with communicating his emotions. He's known Rachel his entire life. They all went to the same high school, and he dated her sister, so there's no way he's not hurting over the unavoidable loss he's about to experience. She only wishes he would admit it and spend some time with Rach before she's gone. Linnea was young, but she remembers him behaving the same way when his parents were sick. He simply pretended it wasn't happening and avoided any conversations to the contrary.

"Okay, sweetheart," Kim says, her gaze rising, only to be met with the back of Mike's head as he leaves the kitchen.

"How are you doing with all of this?" she asks, turning her attention to Linnea. "Honestly, give me the truth."

"It was hard when Grandma and Grandpa died, but I also knew that they wouldn't live forever; everyone loses their grandparents. It's hard not to think of how unfair it all is . . . Rachel dying so young. I try not to talk like that in front of her. She's been in my dreams a lot lately, but in the dreams she's healthy and she tells us it was all a joke. Dr. Lam was in on it, and she doesn't have cancer at all. We aren't even mad at her because we're just so happy she's going to be okay. But, by the end of the dream, we all seem to realize that she *is* sick and has to go. It's so strange."

Linnea takes the napkin that's folded in half next to her empty plate from lunch and wipes her eyes. "I just go in circles; one day I've accepted everything that's happening and the next day I'm just so angry. I think today I'm just tired."

Kim squeezes her daughter's hand. Watching your sister get sicker one day at a time is a gut punch; watching your only child's heart break over the ordeal is torture. Kim's always been a fixer, but there's not a damn thing she can do in this situation, and it's killing her. She only wishes Mike would be a little more present when Linny is hurting. She needs to be able to lean on family in the coming days or weeks; however much time they have left with Rachel.

Dr. Lam emerges from Rachel's room and closes the door behind him. He joins the women at the table, setting his medical bag on the empty chair next to him.

"I've given Rachel a mild sedative, along with a new prescription for the pain. What she needs now is rest, but as you know, it's hard to convince her of that. She'll be spending more time in bed in the coming weeks, so it's important that we get her up and moving whenever possible, or at least rotated so that bed sores don't become an issue. She's experiencing a mild case of constipation, which I anticipate will get worse in the next few days. I've written down a few over-the-counter medicines you might pick up for her at the store this week. If that doesn't help, call me. She's really lucky to be at home with a family who loves her so much. You're both doing a great job; I hope you know that."

Those last few words cause Kim and Linnea to suck in their breaths and let out a sob at the same time. The silver lining is that the mirrored actions get mild laughter from everyone at the table.

"Sorry, this is just so hard," Kim says in a whisper. Her intention is that Rachel never overhear her admitting that caretaking for her terminally ill sister is anything but a walk in the park.

"Of course it is," Dr. Lam says. "She's your only sister. There's no situation in which this is an easy process, even for the strongest of caregivers. All I can tell you is that she is so incredibly fortunate to have such a loving home to live out her final days. I'm sure you can imagine how being in a medical facility would be an entirely different experience for her."

"What else can we do?" Linnea asks, her voice smaller than she intended. "I want to make sure we're doing everything we can."

Dr. Lam's smile is so sympathetic, it nearly sends Linnea over the edge. She feels like a foolish child for even asking. Of course there's nothing she can do to make it easier. She just wants so badly for that to be the case. She wants him to tell her there's this magic thing she can do to make this entire process painless for everyone, especially Rachel.

"Linnea, you're a very good niece. I don't think my nieces and nephews would put in half the effort if it was me in that bed. They'd be too busy on TikTok or playing video games. You're doing everything to the best of your ability; just make sure you're not neglecting the other areas of your life. Your friends, your schoolwork—I know Rachel has mentioned several times that she's been worried you'd fall behind in school because you're spending too much time with her."

"If I don't spend all the time I can with her, I'll regret it for the rest of my life," Linnea fires back immediately.

"I understand that. Just try to find a healthy balance. That's my best advice." Dr. Lam stands and gathers his things, shaking both women's hands as he departs. "You have my number," he says. "Please call me if there is any significant shift in her condition. My office is right down the road, and I can move things around in my schedule to fit her in."

"I know you don't do this for everyone. I can't tell you how grateful we all are for you."

He pauses at the front door, turning to face the women. "When I was getting my undergraduate degree, I couldn't find a job that would work around my school schedule. Your parents put me on as a bag boy at their grocery store and let me choose my hours. When my parents were disappointed in me because I received an A-, rather than an A+ in one of my classes, your parents celebrated my good grades with a cake as I clocked in for my next shift. When the acceptance letter arrived for med school, I told your parents the news before I told my own. Your mom even sent me care packages when I moved to Ann Arbor. There's not a thing I wouldn't do for this family. That's a promise."

As he leaves and Linnea closes the door behind him, it hits Kim—she and her sister were raised with the most caring, wonderful family, and in the coming weeks, she's about to be the last one standing.

Eighteen

"I'M HERE," Linnea whispers as Rachel opens her eyes. She squeezes her aunt's hand.

"Where the fuck else would you be?" Rachel groans, reaching up to itch her face. "Did you think I was dead? Grow up."

Linnea rolls her eyes and drops Rachel's hand back down to the bed. Rachel had slept past dinner and all through the night, and Linnea really felt like this may be the end. Luckily, her aunt's smart mouth is still alive and well.

"He must have gave me the good stuff, eh?"

"Yeah, he must have," Linnea says with a sigh. "Let's get you to the bathroom before you pee all over yourself. You've been horizontal for at least sixteen hours, and I don't feel like washing your sheets."

"You're the worst caregiver I've had. Where's my patient survey? I'm rating you one star. Horrible attitude, do not recommend."

"We both know I'm five-star worthy, Rach."

"Yeah, maybe on a scale of a hundred."

Rachel props herself up on her elbows and slowly maneuvers to a sitting position, swinging her legs off the side of the bed. Once her feet hit the floor, it takes a few moments to orientate herself and she's standing, slowly making her way to the bathroom with Linnea holding her left arm for the duration of the fifteen steps or so it takes to make it to the doorway.

"Do you want me to come in with you?" Linnea asks.

Rachel waves her away. "We aren't to the ass-wiping stage yet, Linny."

Rachel shuts the door behind her, and Linnea laughs as she hears her aunt urinating for what seems like forever, reminding her of the scene in *Austin Powers* where he has an endless stream of urine after being cryogenically frozen for years.

"Evacuation complete," Linnea whispers to herself when she hears the toilet flush.

"What's for dinner?" Rachel asks when she emerges from the bathroom and accepts Linnea's assistance to make it back to the bed.

"Well, seeing as how it's eight o'clock in the morning, how about we tackle breakfast first?"

Rachel gasps. "It's morning? I thought you were kidding about me being out for sixteen hours. What the hell did he give me?"

Linnea snorts and walks over to the window, thrusting open the thick curtains. "We didn't ask, we just trusted that your ass needed to be knocked out for a while. Do you feel rested?"

Rachel considers this. "Yeah, actually. I feel good. I feel hungry, which I suppose is a good sign."

"I'd have to agree. I've had bagel sandwiches on my mind since you told me about you and Rainey eating them all the time in college. How about I go grab us a few?"

"How about I pay and go along for the ride?"

Linnea's eyebrows rise. "Really? You feel well enough? Should I ask Mom?"

Rachel waves her hand forward, dismissing the idea. "I'm forty-one years old. I don't need to ask your mom for permission. My keys are on the hook next to the door. You might as well get used to driving my Volvo—I'm leaving it to you."

Linnea gasps. "Really?"

"Now don't go killing me over an all-wheel drive vehicle that's two years old. I'll be dead soon enough anyway. Now, let's go. I'm dying for a ham, egg, and cheese sandwich. Maybe we'll even get your mom something."

* * *

AFTER GRABBING breakfast from a local drive-thru, Rachel instructs Linnea to park her car down at the beach, facing the water.

"Will you turn up the heat a little?" she asks, shivering.

Linnea stops herself from cracking a joke about Rachel being cold on such a warm summer day when she already has a fleece jacket on. She can't imagine the symptoms she's dealing with, and being unnaturally cold is likely one of the easier side effects while dying of cancer.

"Of course," Linnea says, reaching forward to adjust the vents in Rachel's direction and presses a button to turn on her heated seat.

They sit in silence, Linnea drinking her iced vanilla latte and Rachel her hot chamomile tea. Her aunt can't seem to stomach the entire bagel, so she picks it apart and eats what she can. Her eyes dance on the horizon of Lake Michigan before her. On this early summer morning, the water is in all its glory, perfectly still and sparkling.

"We're so lucky to live here," Rachel whispers.

"Yes, we are," Linnea responds, even though she's guilty of taking this place for granted. She's never lived in a town without miles of vast lake shorelines, vibrantly green forests, and autumns so beautiful that tourists pay just to see the leaves when they change colors. She can't imagine a life without it all surrounding her on a daily basis.

Linnea watches Rachel as she gazes out over the blueish green water. Although she's underweight and her skin has lost its signature glow, she's still stunning. Growing up, Linnea's male friends always gave her hell for having a "hot aunt" and she'd roll her eyes, but damn if they weren't right. Even more importantly, Rachel has always been smart. Fierce. Protective. Independent. She's the kind of woman Linnea hopes to be. Well, minus the random vigilante murdering.

"Rach, why didn't you ever get married?"

Rachel turns slowly, the back of her head not leaving the leather head rest. The corners of her lips curl slightly.

"Did I ever tell you about the time I got engaged?"

"No way," Linnea responds, wondering why her parents never told her.

"Yep. Right before you were born. I guess now is as good a time as any to tell you about him. His name was Lance. This story doesn't have much of a happy ending, but I suppose none of the stories I've been telling you seem to."

"I'm sure you have some stories that have happy endings."

"I sure do, kid. But this ain't one of them."

Nineteen

TWENTY-TWO IS NOT the age to get married, in my humble, elder-millennial opinion. But have you ever tried telling that to a twenty-two-year-old?

I met Lance a week after moving to my new apartment after graduation. The apartment was one bedroom, one bath, and zero charm. Sadly, it was all I could afford with my first entry-level job out of college. The entire complex had a reputation for housing young professionals who might not have a credit score, but most of our parents were happy to help with the deposit if it meant we weren't moving back in with them. We didn't have any money, we didn't have any kids, and we sure as hell didn't have anything better to do on the weekends than sit by the apartment complex's crappy cement pool and drink cheap liquor out of red plastic cups, despite the numerous posted signs forbidding it.

Everyone in the complex seemed to know Lance before I was formally introduced because he was the life of the party. Even on the nights that the crowd said they didn't feel like playing drinking games, he'd have everyone lined up for flip-cup or beer pong within the hour. He knew how to get us up out of our seats after a long week of work. Wearing a hard hat with two cupholders and straws going into his mouth, or a politically incorrect Halloween costume that made everyone laugh, or telling the best bonfire stories—he was just *that* guy. Another good piece of advice for someone that age would be "Don't marry the life of the party," but I didn't have anyone giving me that warning before I fell in love with Lance.

I'm not sure I even loved him as much as I loved the energy that surrounded him. The party didn't start until he arrived. He seemed to know the cashiers at every liquor store within a five-mile radius and could get us the best deals on kegs. He went to trade school to be a mechanic and was a damn good one; he was always underneath one of our cars in the parking lot, fixing it for the price of parts and happy to accept a few beers as payment for the labor.

After being surrounded by (and participating in) binge drinking for four years at Central, I was over it. I became more of a cocktail-or-two-after-work kind of gal, but Lance was still in his peak drinking era, usually cracking a beer open after work before his car was even in park. Looking back now, it's hard to say what I saw in him, but the best way I can explain is that he made me feel special. He was the guy everyone knew, everyone wanted to be around—and he wanted me. When people found out I was dating Lance, their smiles would grow wider as they said things like, "Lance is *the man.*"

He started staying over at my apartment so often, we decided it would be best financially for him to just move in and pay half of the rent. That was the plan, anyway. Each month when the first rolled around, he always had some sort of excuse about why he was going to be a few dollars short with his half. Those nights, he always knew to be a little sweeter to me, pay me a few more compliments, and it worked. I looked past his delinquent bills and helped him cover whatever amount he was short. If my dad knew, he would have slapped me upside the head for being so foolish. He warned me about boys like this my entire life, but somehow Lance seemed different. I made excuses for him all the time. He wasn't a deadbeat; he was just stretched thin. He was doing his best.

He had his faults, but it never crossed my mind that he'd cheat on me. Anytime we hung out with the other twenty-somethings in the complex, he was all over me. He couldn't get enough. He always said he liked to show me off because I was so *damn pretty* and he couldn't believe his luck that I chose him. Yet another bit of advice for women that age: Don't let flattery cloud your judgement.

I suppose that's why I'll never forget the first time it happened. Men had surprised me with their bad behavior in the past, but never like this. I understood the phrase "gut punch" the day I found out he was living a double life.

She lived in the apartments and knew Lance from trade school. She worked in the enrollment office, and their paths apparently crossed before they both moved here. It was a stormy night in late fall, and we were all playing a heated game of beer pong in the basement level of one of the build-ings. Lance was hammered, as usual, and had his hands all over me. He'd kiss me every time he sunk a shot and slap my ass when I did the same. Everyone was having a good time, except for this girl. I couldn't help but feel like she was staring at me. Not just staring, but scowling. She only uncrossed her arms to take a sip of her beer, but never took her eyes from the spot where I was standing. *What in the world did she have against me?*

While we were deciding who was up next, I went over to the cooler to grab myself a beer and I heard her approach Lance and ask about Jinx. His sweet black cat died shortly before he moved in with me. How did this girl know about Jinx—had she been in his apartment before? I took my time retrieving the beer and then fiddled around in my purse to kill time so I could eavesdrop. Their voices lowered so I couldn't make out the words, but her tone became curt. She was irritated with him.

That's the intuition that we ignore when we're young and foolish—that feeling deep in your gut that's telling you something isn't right.

I ignored that feeling for weeks. I seemed to see her everywhere—in the apartment laundry room, in the parking lot, in the gym. I ignored it until I couldn't anymore, and that moment came the day she knocked on my apartment door while Lance was working late to let me know she was pregnant. If Lance didn't pay for the abortion, she was going to go straight to his parents and let them know that they'd be having their first grandchild out of wedlock. I had met Lance's parents by this point, and they would have been devastated. They seemed like good people, but they were very active in their church, and no doubt would be wrecked by whatever their congregation had to say about it.

I got out my checkbook and, with shaking hands, I made it out for the entire amount. She accepted it without a word. I didn't see her as the villain; she looked as devastated as I felt. She moved out of the apartment community shortly after that, and I never saw her again. I'm not sure if Lance could say the same.

When confronted about it, it was like a page out of the

young cheating man's handbook—he called her crazy. He said she was a liar. He told me she'd been in love with him for months and was basically a stalker at this point. Again, deep down I'm sure I knew it wasn't true, but I stayed anyway.

Twenty

HE PROPOSED to me the next fall at an Aerosmith concert. The band had no significance in our relationship that would warrant a proposal at their show; I only knew their major hits that were played on the radio, and Lance had won the tickets from a local radio station giveaway. After mumbling yes, I immediately ran to the bathroom of the arena and got violently ill. I wasn't even drinking. Now, I think my body was trying to warn me it was a bad idea. I should have listened.

By that time, we were renting a small two-bedroom house that didn't even have road access—you had to drive down a narrow, poorly lit alley just to get to it. I'll always remember that house as the backdrop for some of the worst days of my life.

It started with the disrespect he'd show his mother. I'm sure we'd all heard the warning that you should never marry a man who doesn't treat his mother right, but again, I ignored it. I told myself they have years of history that I know nothing about, and maybe she isn't the kind, generous woman I knew her to be. He'd ignore her calls for weeks and answer with a shout of "WHAT?" when he finally picked up. He would chastise me for wanting to spend fifty dollars to send her flowers for Mother's Day, telling me it was a waste of money. He refused to give me any guidance when I wanted to pick out gifts for her birthday or Christmas. Being so close to my own mother, I just couldn't imagine that kind of dynamic. That woman gave him life, and he treated her like an inconvenience.

I'm not sure if it happened overnight or gradually over the months, but he began to treat me exactly as he did his mother. He'd ignore my calls and texts, act as if I was a nuisance for asking him what he'd like for dinner, refuse to do anything together as a couple. Lance was no longer the life of the party. He was a permanently angry twenty-something who only smiled when he was hanging out with his core group of friends, who were also mechanics.

One of the friends was a decade or so older than us and could afford a very spacious shop on his property, so that's where the guys all hung out. They'd sit in camping chairs around a small gas firepit, drinking and telling stories until the wee hours of the morning, when he would call me to come pick him up. He was surprisingly reasonable about not drinking and driving, which is about the nicest thing I can say about Lance.

No matter what I had going on the next day or how early I had to be at the office, I always picked him up. Two, three, four in the morning—you wouldn't hear a complaint out of me. I was just so thankful he wasn't getting behind the wheel of his Jeep after a night of drinking.

The first time (that I'm aware of) he cheated after we were engaged was over a long holiday weekend. It was Labor Day, and I had gotten the call that one of my aunts most likely had hours or days to live, so I got in the car to drive up to my hometown in the Upper Peninsula to see her and say my goodbyes. Lance didn't come because he "only met her a few times" and didn't want to miss out on the lake trip he had planned with his friends and their wives, as they'd already paid for their spot at the campground. Wouldn't want to be out twenty-five dollars so he could be by his future-wife's side while she said goodbye to her favorite aunt, right? What an inconvenience that would have been.

The first thing I remember about that weekend is hearing from one of his friend's wives on Friday night, shortly after I arrived in my hometown. All the wives were there, and when they asked why I didn't show up, Lance shrugged and told them I just didn't feel like it. He didn't tell them about the loss my family was suffering or why I had to leave town—he let them believe I just didn't want to come.

Throughout the weekend, Lance didn't check in on me. He didn't respond to any of my texts or calls. I noticed a charge on my debit card for a restaurant on the lake for nearly a hundred dollars. I wasn't stupid—he'd paid for someone else's meal along with his own.

This is why I always tell young women to trust their gut; I knew something wasn't right. I knew he was up to no good. While scrolling social media in the middle of the night when I couldn't sleep, I saw a post Lance was tagged in by a female I'd never seen before. It was a picture of him with his arm wrapped around her neck, both in swimsuits, and her tongue sticking out. The caption was "Labor Day? More like BABER Day!" My stomach sank.

My Aunt Cynthia died early Saturday morning. Kim and I both felt relief; she had been bedridden for over a year, and her quality of life was non-existent. There wasn't much for me to do, as her wishes were to be cremated and for there to be no memorial service; she couldn't stand the thought of anyone fussing over her. That's a common theme in our family wills and directives, which is why we haven't had many big funerals.

Sunday afternoon, something told me I needed to get on the road and make the six-hour drive down to the campground where Lance and his friends were staying. I didn't tell him I was coming; I simply packed up and plugged the address into my GPS.

I got to the lake shortly before sunset, which was normally my favorite time of day. Golden hour—that's when the magic is supposed to happen. This night ruined golden hour for me for a long time.

For the rest of my days, I will never forget how his friends (and their wives, who I thought were my friends, but was mistaken) sat straight up and began darting their eyes around when I got out of my car. Lance was nowhere in sight.

They were sitting in a circle around the campfire and nearly tripped over themselves trying to act casual about where my fiancé was. Nobody had a straight answer for me. The girl from the social media post was also missing from the group.

Within minutes, everyone's attention turned to the lakefront, where a jet ski pulled up and parked on the shore. A couple hopped off. He wrapped a towel around her as they walked toward the campsite, laughing at a joke too low for me to hear.

They stopped dead in their tracks when they saw me standing there. I didn't say a word. The look in her eyes told me that she knew exactly who I was. I took the tiny diamond engagement ring off my finger and set it on the ground in front of me. I didn't throw it. I didn't scream. I didn't cry. I just got in my car and drove home.

Twenty-One

THE FOLLOWING WEEKS WERE HELL. I didn't have the self-confidence to leave him. I know that may seem silly now because I've grown into a woman who doesn't take shit from anyone, and I had already shown I had the strength to stand up when something wasn't right, but back then I made a lot of decisions that didn't make much sense at all. I think every woman goes through a period where she just isn't herself and makes choices like a person she doesn't recognize. I could give great advice to my friends; I just wasn't taking it myself.

For weeks, I had a pain so deep in my stomach I considered going to the hospital several times before talking myself out of it. I couldn't eat. I couldn't sleep. My skin was breaking out like I was a hormonal middle schooler.

Every morning on my commute to work, I'd turn the radio off and drive in silence. I'd daydream about a life in which I never met Lance. I was young, free, and full of hope. I didn't have to worry about telling everyone how many times he'd cheated on me (by this point, I believe we were at number five, but I won't bore you with the details of the others), and I didn't have to face the embarrassment of a

"

failed engagement. I didn't even know his parents that well, but I felt that I'd be letting them down if I left their son. If only I hadn't agreed to marry him, none of this would be so bad. I wouldn't be in so deep. I wept when I thought of the list of family friends and their addresses that his mother had dropped off the week before. She also asked when I'd be free to go to Macy's and create a gift registry.

That year we'd received an impressively large tax return, thanks to the current administration's first-time home buyer's credit, and Lance spent it all on upgrades for his Jeep. Our savings account had just over one hundred dollars in it—the bare minimum amount to keep it open without penalty. How was I going to leave him? I had nothing, and I was terrified to ask my parents for help because I'd have to admit how I got into this situation, and it was much too large of an "I told you so" for me to stomach. Dad had been warning me my entire life to look out for guys like Lance, and what did I do? I'd accepted his marriage proposal. I was just in too deep.

We were cordial to each other at home. He knew he messed up, but he certainly didn't want to talk about it. He wanted to move on with life as normal without his future wife bringing up all the times he'd deceived me. He became a pathological liar. Hell, maybe he always was, and I was just noticing the extent of it, but the lies became ridiculous. He'd forget my birthday, and when I'd politely remind him and let him know how much it hurt my feelings, he would come up with an elaborate story about how he was going to surprise me with a weekend away, but I had ruined it all by acting like a brat, so he'd just cancel it.

One of my coworkers saw him at the jewelry store in the mall one day on his lunch break. When several holidays passed without receiving any jewelry, I'd finally decided to ask him about it. Again, he lost his temper and said that my friends need to mind their own business, and if I had just a little more patience, I would have found out that he bought me a bracelet and was going to gift it to me for Valentine's Day . . . which was ten months after he was seen in the jewelry store. This man didn't remember to purchase gifts for holidays at all, let alone have the forethought to pre-purchase them ten months prior.

I could go on about the lies, but they were all the same. Each one more asinine than the last and all of them ending with anger and denial on his end, successfully shifting the blame on me for catching him in the lie.

I had a feeling he was cheating again, and it was all but confirmed one day while he was at work at the shop. He sent me a selfie of his body, naked from the waist down, in the bathroom at work. I gasped at the graphic angle of the picture. Lance and I had never sent each other nude pictures; we'd never even discussed it. We didn't talk dirty to each other via text or on the phone. I was twenty-three and quite naïve in that department—when I had my wild days in college, it was in the early days of social media, and we were still using flip phones. After a few minutes of silence, he sent me a text trying to play it off like it was meant for me. I wondered if he ended up sending the same picture to the girl it was meant for, or if he had the decency to take a new one for her.

I was at my wit's end. Each night I'd get home from work, cook him dinner, and eat in silence while he played on his phone. I'd then pour myself a bath and sob while the water ran so he couldn't hear me. There just had to be some-thing more to life than this. That's what I kept telling myself.

A small lifeline was thrown to me in early spring when my company asked me to travel to southern Illinois to oversee the acquisition of a smaller organization there. I accepted without hesitation. I needed a change of scenery and a break from Lance. Our household had become so depressing.

The night before I left for my trip, I let Lance know that I'd need to be on the road by six the next morning to make it to the facility in time for my first meeting. He told me he was going to drink at the shop with the boys, and I again reminded him of how early I needed to get up and how important it was that I was rested for this trip. He promised he wouldn't be late, and either wouldn't drink enough to require a ride, or he'd call me early enough to pick him up and still get a full night's sleep.

I'm sure it comes as no surprise when I tell you he didn't keep his promise. I checked in with a text at nine, ten, again at eleven—no response. Midnight came and went without a word from Lance. I knew I wouldn't be able to fall asleep without knowing he was okay, so I lay awake, staring at the ceiling, my packed suitcase already in the trunk of my car.

I managed to doze off for an hour or so and awoke at nearly two in the morning in a panic—I flipped over to his side of the bed and found it empty. What started as concern switched to rage. I couldn't believe he was doing this to me. He knew how important this trip was to me and how it was the first time my boss was trusting me to lead such a big project.

I didn't even bother changing out of my pajamas when I hopped in my car and drove the eight miles to his friend's shop. Sure enough, the driveway was filled with familiar cars, and I could see the flickering light of the gas firepit from the largest bay. I parked behind the last car and hiked up the gravel drive in my pink fuzzy slippers. Roaring laughter could be heard from across the property, and I wondered what this man's neighbors thought of these rowdy get-togethers that lasted well into the early hours of the morning.

I stomped into the shop to grab Lance and stopped in my tracks. While his friends were all in their usual spots, in camping chairs surrounding the fire pit, Lance was leaned back with a female on his lap.

I remember that before anyone realized I was there, I looked at the faces of his friends and none of them seemed concerned that my fiancé had another woman on his lap. It was only when I got a little closer that I realized it wasn't a woman; it was the seventeen-year-old daughter of his boss at the dealership. Seventeen years old. I knew this because Lance showed me the pictures of the car her father bought her the year before, for her sixteenth birthday.

I was at a loss for words. Not only was he cheating again, but she was a minor. His friends were all seemingly okay with it. He had the decency to throw her off his lap when he saw me, but the damage had been done. I felt like I was going to be sick, but I didn't want to give him the satisfaction.

I turned on my heels, got in my car, and drove. I stopped at home to grab the last of my things for the trip and hit the road by three. Back then, they sold these tiny bottles at gas stations that had enough caffeine to keep a three-hundred-pound trucker awake for days. I had two on my way to Illinois.

I arrived at the job, spent the day closing the acquisition deal, and never spoke to Lance again.

Twenty-Two

"WHAT DO you mean you never spoke to him again? Didn't you have to go back and move your things out and deal with the breakup? Whatever happened with the girl—did you turn him in for having relations with a minor?"

Linnea is asking questions so rapidly, her brain can barely keep up. Rachel simply smiles and returns her gaze to the lake in front of them. She pulls the zipper on her jacket up high to her chin after a chill hits her.

"Would you believe that while I was in Illinois, that tiny little rental house we had exploded? Apparently, the wiring wasn't exactly up to code and a fire broke out. When it reached the propane tank in our garage—boom. The entire property gone, even his stupid Jeep. And poor Lance was sleeping off another night of poor decisions, so he probably never saw it coming. It was such a tragedy."

Rachel picks at her nail polish before shrugging and taking a sip of her tea. Although she's looking forward, she can see Linnea's eyes grow wide in her peripheral.

"Rachel, you didn't . . ."

Rachel furrows her brow and cocks her head. "Didn't what?" She smiles.

"Oh my god," Linnea whispers.

"What do you think should happen to a grown man who messes with a girl that is barely old enough to drive?"

Linnea moves her gaze to the lake. She doesn't want to say it out loud, but her first thought was, *He should die.* "I'm not sure," she answers instead.

"Look, I'm not entirely innocent in this. After the fourth or fifth time he cheated on me, I ended up having an emotional affair with a man who delivered paper supplies to my office. I left that out of the story."

"What's an emotional affair?"

Rachel considers her words before responding. "I'm not sure everyone's definition would be the same, but for me it was a situation where I started to seek comfort in another man. He's the one who asked about my day. He's the one who sent a condolence bouquet when my aunt died. He's the only one I felt truly understood me. If he lived closer, I can't tell you it wouldn't have been a physical affair. Maybe I'm no better than Lance was. Every time he pissed me off or disappointed me, I'd reach for my phone to text the other guy. He always answered, and he always talked to me until the hurt faded away."

Linnea huffs. "Aunt Rachel, I'd say what you did was a little different than what this Lance guy did."

"Hey, I promised you I'd tell you everything—the good, bad, and the ugly. Carrying on with that man wasn't a decent thing to do, and I'll be the first to admit it. But I suppose I did love him, and he represented a different ending to my story— he was the kind of man I should have chosen. My life would be much different if I had."

"So whatever happened with him? Did you date after Lance died?"

Rachel turns to Linnea and smiles. "Nah, we could never seem to get the timing right. He ended up marrying a girl from his hometown. His name is Eddie, and he may have moved on, but I'll never forget him."

"Does he know you're . . ."

"Dying?"

Linnea nods uncomfortably.

"Nope. I'd rather he remember me young and beautiful. Maybe I'll leave him a note, like the one I'm leaving you. I'll give you his full name so you know how to track him down and get him the letter when I'm gone. Deal?"

"Deal," Linnea says with a nod. "But I sure wish you'd contact him now. I bet he'd like to say goodbye."

"I'll think about it," Rachel lies.

"What about your other friends? Mom says they've been contacting her because they can't get you to return their texts. Don't you think they deserve to spend some time with you?"

Rachel isn't sure how to answer this. Technically, Linnea is an adult, but it doesn't mean she's matured enough to understand all the little nuances that come with this situation. Hell, Rachel is in her forties and has a hard time wrapping her mind around everything that has happened in the last year. A few of her childhood best friends still live in the area, but they are busy with their own lives. They have kids, full-time jobs, and households to run. She doesn't want to be a burden. She also doesn't want them to remember her this way. She's always been the fun friend. The sarcastic, high-energy, optimistic friend. Now she's dying and she's not sure how much optimism she can muster. The song and dance she performs for Linnea is almost enough to push her over the edge with exhaustion; she can't imagine having to keep it up in front of an entire list of old friends.

"I'm going to see if they want to stop by next week. The weather is supposed to be nice; maybe we can sit out on the back deck and get some sunshine."

This seems to pacify Linnea enough to put the car in reverse and begin the drive home.

"Are you worried I'm going to tell Mom the things you've confessed?" she asks once they turn into the neighborhood. Rachel can tell the question has been weighing on Linnea.

"Not for a minute," Rachel answers, honestly. "We have a bond that I'd never doubt, and I think we both know how special that is."

"What about after you're gone?"

"After I'm gone, you can tell her whatever you'd like, kid. I won't be here to stop you."

Twenty-Three

RACHEL KEEPS her promise the following week and invites her three best childhood friends over. The last time they saw each other was shortly before her diagnosis, when they met up at the beach and gossiped for hours while consuming entirely too many of those little frozen daquiri pouches that you can buy at the Quick Stop. They complained about their kids, and Rachel complained about her random aches and pains. She wonders if they replay that afternoon in their minds—Rachel telling them she can barely get out of bed some days due to her lower back pain and them assuring her that it was just a part of turning forty.

Now she sits on the back deck of her sister's house with a blanket wrapped around her shoulders despite the pleasant temperature, and the realization that they should have done this a lot sooner, before her body was showing so many signs of her deteriorating health. God bless these women, as they are doing their best to pretend everything is normal and that they haven't noticed the weight loss, pale skin, or sunken cheekbones. They knew she had terminal cancer, yet none of them expected it to take its toll so quickly. The women are taking turns asking her questions while speaking slowly and loudly, as if they assume she must be suffering hearing loss along with her drastically changed appearance.

"You know, the cancer hasn't spread to my ear drums," Rachel says in an even tone, mustering a wry smile.

Her friend Sophia blushes and begins to apologize. Rachel cuts her off.

"Guys, it's me. The same girl you gave shit to for wearing a gold-colored jumpsuit to the sixth-grade Christmas program and kissing Jackson Symanski under the bleachers until my braces cut his lip open junior year. You don't have to handle me with kid gloves. I'm dying, and all I ask is that you help me feel normal for however long I have left here. Stop coddling me. I love you guys, but stop."

After a few beats of silence, her friend Monica clears her throat and says, "Okay, you little bitch."

All four women erupt in laughter. Rachel is wheezing, tears cascading down her cheeks. She can't remember the last time she felt this good, despite the shooting pain in her side each time she sucks in another breath to laugh.

Rachel internally cheers when all three women honor her request and begin treating her normally again. They sit on the deck for over an hour, telling stories about their heyday and pulling long forgotten inside jokes from the depths of their recollections. Each time one of the women brings up a memory the others had lost, an avalanche of laughter nearly knocks them out of their patio chairs. The clouds have parted enough for the sun to shine directly on Rachel's cheeks, and she drops the blanket from her shoulders. She's stopped shivering for the first time in what feels like weeks.

This, Rachel thinks. *This is what it's all about, isn't it? This is the high we chase our whole lives.*

"God, I'm starving. Should we order food?" Sophia asks, and Rachel smiles at the fact that she, too, is hungry.

On cue, Kim swings open the patio door and announces that she ordered a few pizzas, and they are on the way. They all offer to pay, and Kim waves them away. She'd pay ten times the amount of that pizza bill to continue hearing her little sister laugh like this. She was afraid she'd never hear that glorious sound again. Kim wants to hug each of the women tightly around their necks and thank them for bringing her sister back to life, if only for one night, but she plays it cool. She doesn't want to ruin Rachel's good time by acting overly emotional. Instead, she goes in the house and retrieves a stack of paper plates and napkins for the women, setting the stack on the patio table between them and vowing to come back out once the pizzas arrive.

Inside, Linnea sits at the dining room table working on a five-hundred-piece puzzle she picked up at the thrift store the day before.

"That puzzle is used—what are you going to do if it's missing a piece?" Kim asks.

"Say a few cuss words and flip this table over in a fit of rage."

Kim gasps. "Linnea Jane, you wouldn't dare."

Linnea sets the piece she's holding back down on the table and takes a deep breath. "Mom, you've got to lighten up. You've got to learn to take a joke. I know things are really heavy right now, but you just have to get that stick out of your butt and enjoy life while you can."

"Linnea!"

"Mom."

"I can tell your aunt is rubbing off on you. I might need to have a talk with her."

Kim closes her cardigan tightly around her body, which

makes Linnea laugh because it's her mother's version of clutching her pearls. *God, when will this woman lighten up?*

"I'm lucky to be spending time with Aunt Rachel. Do you even know what a badass she is?"

Kim takes a seat at the table next to her daughter, giving her a tight smile that doesn't travel far past her lips. "A badass, huh? And what makes you say that about my bratty little sister?"

Linnea wants to grab her shoulders and shout, "Oh, I don't know, maybe because she's been taking justice into her own hands her entire life and protecting the rest of us from horrible men? Maybe because she always does what's right? Or how about the fact that she's strong enough to have bared the weight of these unimaginable secrets her entire life until now?" Linnea cannot imagine the silent struggle Rachel has fought for decades. She's the strongest person Linnea has ever known, and it breaks her heart to know that her reputation is going to be tarnished the minute the confession letter is delivered to the authorities after her passing.

"She just is, Mom. She's the kind of person you want in your corner when shit hits the fan, you know?"

Kim smiles. "Well, I can't argue with that."

"Pizza here yet?" Mike says, peeking his head in through the kitchen door that leads to the garage.

"No, dear, but you could come in here and help your daughter with this puzzle until it gets here."

Mike inhales and prepares an excuse before his eyes land on his only daughter and he thinks better of it. "Let me wash the grease off my hands."

Linnea raises her eyebrows when the door closes behind him. "What makes you think I want his help?"

Kim rubs her arm. "He won't be of much help at all, but at least he'll be spending time with us."

Linnea loves her dad, but it's infuriating that her mom is constantly having to beg him to do the bare minimum. She never noticed it much growing up because it's how everyone's dads act around here. They work full-time and then come home and piddle around with house projects until their favorite football team, baseball team, or NASCAR driver is on TV. That's when they crack open a beer and sit in their recliners, where they doze off until it's time to stumble to the bedroom. They then repeat that pattern until they are lying on their death beds and wishing they'd spent more time with their families and less time working.

It was not until she met the fathers of her fellow class-mates during her freshman year at college and observed their active involvement in their children's lives that she realized the upbringing she and her friends experienced was not typi-cal. There *were* dads out there who spent time with their kids and made sacrifices for the happiness of the family.

The sound of the garage fridge closing and the top of an aluminum can opening signifies that Mike is actually going to take a break and join the women. After entering through the kitchen door, he turns his head sharply as a fresh batch of laughter sounds from the deck outside.

"What's going on out there, spring break?"

"Rachel's just catching up with the girls. You remember them from the neighborhood, right? Sophia, Monica, and Jen?" Kim asks.

"Nice of them to finally show up," Mike mutters before taking a seat across from his daughter.

Linnea jumps to defend her aunt without hesitation. "They've been trying to contact her for months. Rachel has been having a hard time with the whole thing, so she hasn't been easy to get ahold of. I can't say I blame her. I wouldn't want my friends to remember me like that, either. Nobody wants to be remembered by their final weeks."

"Final weeks?" Mike asks. "You think she's only got weeks left?"

Neither Kim nor Linnea wants to be the one to answer the question. Reluctantly, Kim speaks up. "Her latest scans weren't great, babe. Dr. Lam seems to think we are talking about a matter of weeks rather than months now."

For the first time, Linnea detects genuine sorrow in her dad's eyes. She so often thinks of this impending loss as only belonging to her and her mother, but her dad has known Rachel for most of his life. This can't be easy on him. He's just not great at showing emotion, so Linnea forgets how hard this is going to be for him, as well.

"Do you have any fun Rachel stories? I was just telling Mom what a badass I think she is."

"A badass, huh?" Mike says, the left corner of his lip curling into a crooked smirk. "No, sweetheart. She was just your mom's pain-in-the-butt little sister, so my friends and I didn't spend too much time around her growing up. I guess I wish that was different now."

Linnea watches her mom as her father speaks, and she sees her brows slightly furrow at the words. What an odd answer to her question, Linnea thinks. He's known Rachel for decades. All these years with her and he can't think of a single story to tell?

Twenty-Four

MIRACULOUSLY, Rachel feels well enough by the weekend to make it down to the half-finished basement to watch a so-called feel-good movie, which Kim assured her would make all of life's worries disappear for a night. Kim's own worries currently include ensuring that Rachel is comfortable (yes, she has been the thirteen times Kim has asked so far), that the girls have enough snacks (yes, Rachel and Linnea say the selection is bordering on overkill), and that Mike will be okay upstairs on his own for a few hours while the women have their movie night. Yes, Rachel's sister must make sure that her middle-aged, perfectly healthy husband can survive on his own in a fully stocked kitchen and furnished house for two to three hours on his own. She'd make a sarcastic comment, but this damn disease is stealing the wise-cracking energy directly from her soul.

Rachel leans toward Linnea and speaks in a low, conspiratorial tone when Kim makes "one last trip" upstairs to check on Mike before the movie begins. They already have the film cued up and paused on the MGM Studios opening graphic, ready to go.

"You know your dad is a man-child, right?"

Linnea doesn't bother arguing. "Which makes Mom an enabler, yeah?"

Rachel nods and bites off the end of a Twizzler. "The biggest. That's awfully mature of you to recognize it. I didn't know what the fuck an enabler was at your age."

"Were they always like this?" Linnea asks.

Rachel swivels her head to face her niece. "Mike's always been kind of a jerk, and your mom has always been kind of a pushover, so I suppose it was a match made in heaven. It's just gotten worse over the years. Your mom's backbone has completely disappeared."

"It's weird getting to an age where I recognize that my dad is kind of a jerk. When I was a kid, I thought he was a hero."

Rachel huffs and then holds her hands up in apology for the reaction to Mike being called a hero.

"You don't really hate my dad, though, do you?" Linnea asks.

Rachel takes a beat too long to respond, which tells Linnea the answer, regardless of what Rachel is about to say. "Nah, kid. I don't hate your dad. He gets on my nerves, but that's what family is for, right? We have a long history, and I don't think of him as my sister's husband. I think of him as someone who has been around for as long as I can remember. Of course we are going to have our differences. I just love Kim and want what's best for her, always. I'm sure I over-react a little when I feel like she's not being treated very well. Hey, I've told you how I've stuck up for women in the past when they were treated like dirt. I keep my guard up when it comes to protecting people I love."

Before Linnea can reply, they are interrupted by the sound

of Kim's footsteps as she descends the carpeted stairs to the basement.

"Okay, ladies, are we ready?"

"I don't know, did you check Mike's diaper first, or is he good for a few hours?"

Kim tsks. "You're so hateful."

Rachel shrugs and takes another bite of her Twizzler.

* * *

SHE'S NOT willing to admit it out loud, but Kim was right—the movie was the perfect distraction. For two hours and twenty-two minutes, Rachel managed to forget that she was in her final months (or *weeks*?) of her life here on earth. She laughed, she cried, she felt so deeply for the characters, she forgot about being the main character in her own story, which is nearing its final act.

"Did you guys ever go to a summer camp?" Linnea asks, inspired by the wooded, lakeside setting of the movie.

Kim and Rachel roar with laughter at the question.

"Do you want to be the one to tell her, or should I?" Kim asks.

"It's my shame; I'll own it," Rachel responds, sitting up a little straighter on the couch, where Kim has her surrounded by at least five overstuffed pillows, as if she's a toddler in danger of falling over. She has too much pride to admit how comfortable it was for the duration of the movie. If the movie wasn't so damn good, she probably would have fallen asleep.

"So, your mom wanted to go to this summer camp in Iron County her entire childhood. At first, our parents said no because they couldn't afford it. Then, they slowly started making enough money to set some aside for Kim to go to summer camp, but they felt bad about doing it for one daughter and not the other. But the kicker was, I didn't want to go. Kim begged me to change my mind because it was either both of us or neither—going to camp was a packaged deal.

"Finally, in 1999, I was fifteen years old and realized that there would be boys from other towns at camp and I might find a little summer romance, so I agreed to attend. We were both scheduled for the last session of the summer, in August. Your mom acted like she won the lottery; going to camp would be the best thing that ever happened to her. It's the only thing she talked about all summer long. And then, right before we were set to arrive, two campers died there under mysterious circumstances, and the whole place shut down. She never got to go."

Rachel laughs wickedly while Kim shakes her head.

"Wait, the Shady Oaks murders? Is that what you're talking about?" Linnea asks, eyes darting back and forth between her mother and aunt. "You guys were supposed to go to Shady Oaks?"

"Yes, and I don't see what Rachel could find so hilarious. Two innocent teenagers died, *and* I never got to fulfill my dream of going to a sleepaway camp, all because your aunt is a stubborn mule who was hell-bent on ruining my summer."

"Are you suggesting those kids died because I'm a stubborn mule?" Rachel asks, amused. "Wasn't it ruled a murder-suicide anyway? I can't remember whatever came of it."

Kim slaps her arm a little too hard, and Rachel winces. "Oh my god, I'm so sorry, sis," says Kim. "I am so used to slapping you for your smart mouth, it was a knee-jerk reaction."

Rachel smiles, playing off the pain. "I only winced to make you feel bad for hitting someone on their deathbed. What a monster you are."

Kim shakes her head, once again amazed that her little sister has retained her sense of humor throughout this entire ordeal.

"I'm going to bring all this food that you two didn't eat back upstairs and check on Mike."

"It's not our fault that you prepared enough snacks for a football team, Mom."

Kim is now on her feet, folding the blanket she had on her lap and throwing it on the back of the couch.

"You've been spending too much time with Rachel," Kim says, shooting her sister a look that tells her what she thinks of Linnea's newfound sassiness.

"So you've said," Linnea replies, before she and Rachel break out in laughter.

Kim gathers the rest of the snacks and takes one last glance at the girls before heading back upstairs. They sure are two peas in a pod. It's going to take months of therapy and healing for Linnea to get over the loss she's about to experience, and there's not much Kim can do to make it easier. What a helpless, helpless feeling.

Twenty-Five

"TAKE THE DAMN MEDICINE," Kim says, holding the bottle in Rachel's direction. Rachel turns her head away like a toddler, refusing to look at it.

"I don't need it."

"Rachel, you haven't pooped in days. You need to drink this, or you're going to be in even more pain than you already are."

Rachel side-eyes the bottle and shakes her head again. "Quit paying attention to my bowel movements, you creep."

Kim huffs. "Please."

Rachel exhales so loudly and dramatically, it brings a smile to Kim's lips.

"Fine."

She takes a swig directly from the bottle and swallows.

Kim gasps. "Aren't you going to read the correct dosage first?"

"What's going to happen if I get it wrong? I die?" Rachel says with a level of nonchalance that infuriates her sister.

"You understand that your death is going to rock our worlds, right? You're my only sister. You're Linny's favorite aunt. Nothing about our lives will be the same when you're gone, and you won't stop joking about it."

Rachel leans forward in the bed and grasps her sister's hand. "You've got to have a sense of humor in this life, Kim. Or you'll never make it out alive."

Rachel winks and Kim rolls her eyes. "That doesn't even make any damn sense. What is it that you and Linny have been talking about, anyway? You spend hours in here, and she's always quiet when she leaves. You're not telling her a bunch of depressing nonsense, are you?"

"I'm just making sure she really knows me before I go; that's all."

"Well, that *is* some depressing nonsense," Kim responds with a smile.

Rachel is proud of her. She knows she's trying to lighten up, despite her innate tendencies to be outraged by anything resembling a joke.

"I'm going to go grab some groceries. Anything special you'd like?"

"Some adult diapers for when this laxative hits?" Rachel suggests.

Kim squeezes her arm before standing from the edge of the bed that she's been perched on for an hour, begging Rachel to just take the damn medicine.

"Mike's in the garage if you need anything, and Linny should be home around dinner. I'll have my cell on me if you need me."

"I'll try not to die while you're gone," Rachel says.

Kim gasps like she's going to scold her, but thinks better of it, simply shaking her head as she walks out the door.

* * *

SHORTLY BEFORE DINNER, Linnea pulls into the driveway and smiles when she sees that Rachel's curtains are opened slightly. She knows Rachel only lets the light in when she's having a good day. Bad days are spent in complete darkness, with the occasional light of the en suite bathroom flickering on beneath her closed bedroom door until she feels well enough to ask for food. Rachel treated it as a joke when Kim bought her a small bell a few weeks ago, but she's now found it necessary on the days she has a hard time getting out of bed.

Linnea puts her car in park and squints as she sees movement in Rachel's room. Her mom texted her a while ago to say she was headed to the grocery store, and that's normally a several-hour excursion with all the extra stops she likes to make. So she's not sure who would be moving around Rachel's room. A moment of optimism jolts through her body when she wonders if it could be Rachel, feeling well enough to walk around. Maybe she really is having a good day.

She pulls out her phone to take a video so she can send it to her mom; she knows it would make her day to see that Rachel is feeling well enough to be up and around. Smiling, she holds the screen up and focuses on the window, slowly zooming in. She narrates the scene while she films.

"Mom, I just pulled up to the house, and I think Aunt Rach is up moving around. Let me catch her in her natural habitat," she says, the last sentence morphing into a horribly botched Australian accent. "There's a very good chance the laxatives have hit and she's zooming to the bathroom, but she's on her feet nonetheless."

Linnea nearly drops the phone when she realizes there *is* someone else in her aunt's room because they are much too large to be Rachel. With the phone's camera set at maximum zoom, she lands on the back of a head with short, brown hair that she'd recognize anywhere. Leaned forward in the reading chair where Linnea normally sits, is her father.

Finally, she thinks. *Finally he is spending time with her and making his peace. Maybe he just didn't want Mom and me around while he did it. He's a tough man; he needs privacy before showing emotion.*

She stops recording and sets the phone back down in her lap before her attention is drawn back to the window, where she sees her aunt's arms flailing rapidly. She knows those gestures. Rachel is mad. She's arguing. She's losing her temper. Mike places both hands on the bed and leans forward, as if whispering to Rachel. She holds her finger up inches from Mike's face and delivers a line that makes him stand and place his hands on his hips, shaking his head as he leaves the room. Rachel takes one of the decorative pillows from the bed and throws it across the room, hitting the door frame.

Rachel is on her deathbed. What in the world would they have to argue about?

Twenty-Six

RACHEL ISN'T OFFERING any information, and Linnea isn't asking. She waited in her car for a few more minutes while she took some deep breaths and perfected her utterly clueless I-just-got-here-and-didn't-see-anything act before entering the house.

Her father was back in the garage, and Rachel was in her room with the door shut. Linnea entered cheerfully, as she always does, and pretended not to see the red, inflamed skin under Rachel's eyes.

"How are you feeling today?" Linnea asks as she takes a seat in the reading chair, pretending not to notice that the seat is still warm from her father.

"I'm doing okay today, kiddo. Still haven't used the bathroom, but I feel some magic working in there. Is your mom back yet?"

"Aldi restocked their fun nonsense aisle, so I have a feeling she might be a while. I'm not sure how many porcelain cannisters we need that say sugar on the outside, but I have a hunch that Mom feels it's more than the three already in our kitchen."

Rachel manages a slight smile, but Linnea can tell her mind is somewhere else. How is it that Rachel can share her deepest secrets with Linnea, yet won't tell her about a fight with her father?

"Want to talk?" Linnea offers.

"Sure, Linny. What do you want to talk about?"

"Dealer's choice," she says, leaning back in the chair and kicking her feet up on the ottoman. "Have any more life advice for me today? Confessions of homicide? Old family recipes?"

There's a certain ease that washes over Rachel's expression whenever someone feels comfortable enough to joke while she's in this condition, so Linnea tries to do it as often as possible. Sometimes it even helps Linnea forget what's happening.

"Let me tell you what happens when you get older, kid."

"Uh oh," Linnea responds with an uncomfortable laugh. "If this is about urinary incontinence, I've seen the commercials."

"Hear me out," Rachel begins. "When you're young, there's just so much excitement in your life. You're excited about going to the playground or the amusement park. When you're a teenager, you're so smitten with whatever boy or girl you are in love with that week, it makes your heart beat faster just thinking about them. You're excited about friends, about concerts, about good grades and school dances. And then you go to college and have a whole new set of things to be excited about—parties, new outfits, job offers after graduation. It's just twenty years of pure excitement over things you've never experienced before. And then, as you get older, you begin to get a little jaded by the world around you. You have bills, responsibilities, maybe a family to worry about. That's also when you begin to realize that there's a lot of ugly in the world. It's not just the blatant monsters in plain sight; it's also just miserable people you encounter who want to hurt your spirit for no reason.

"It's like you just blink and one day you're just going through the motions because you're so exhausted by the world around you. You're sick of the ugliness and too tired to do anything about it. You're going to work, keeping the house clean, trying to stay sane. You might watch a few funny videos on your phone before bed, and you realize that's the only damn joy you've felt all day. I'm begging you, Linnea, you can't let that happen to you. You are so smart and so kind, and you can't let the world get you down. Work hard and enjoy your life. Find those things that make your heart beat faster, and don't you ever let them go. You hold onto them for dear life. Don't let the bastards get you down. Don't let your life become dull because some asshole has stolen your light. You always hear people say 'be the change you want to see in the world,' and it's the truth. You want more kindness? Be kind. You want more empathy? Lead by example. Show how easy it is to be a good person, and maybe you'll just inspire others to be better."

Linnea finds herself wiping a tear from under one of her eyes. "Damn, Aunt Rach, you should have given my class's graduation speech."

"I've had a lot of time in this room to think, and I just want to make sure I'm preparing you for life the best that I can and making sure you don't end up with regrets like I have. I blinked and I'm here. I wasted so much time, Linny. I should have been a better person."

Linnea gazes into Rachel's eyes, willing her to understand that the things she's confessed haven't made her love any weaker. Sure, she may have handled things differently, but she's grown to accept the decisions that Rachel has made and certainly understands the intention behind them. At this point, she can't think of a thing Rachel could confess that would change Linnea's mind. She has Rachel's back.

Rachel gazes back, wishing she could prepare Linnea for the things she has yet to say.

Twenty-Seven

SOPHIA, Monica, and Jen are over again, and Kim is overjoyed that Rachel is allowing her childhood friends a proper goodbye. She hid from them for months and, although Kim understands Rachel's hesitation, she's glad that the women who have been around since they were in diapers are getting the closure they deserve. One afternoon of pizza and laughter on the deck just isn't enough time for an adequate goodbye.

Rachel's condition has taken a turn in the last few days, and her energy and hunger levels are both dangerously low. It broke Kim's heart when Dr. Lam informed her that Rachel would quit eating altogether toward the end, when her body starts shutting down and simply "doesn't require" food anymore. For months, Kim has laid in her bed staring at the ceiling and preparing herself to say goodbye to her little sister, but conversations like that hit her like a shot right to her gut.

Kim and Rachel have been close their entire lives. A lot of situations have felt like "us against the world," particularly when they lost both parents within nine months of each other.

Anytime tragedy strikes, Rachel is always the person Kim wants by her side while they grieve. She may annoy Kim with her attempts at humor when it's highly inappropriate, but she's thankful to have a strong-willed sister during the tough times.

The strange thing about Rachel succumbing to cancer—ignoring the symptoms for so long—is that Kim is the one to ignore what's ailing her so she can focus on everyone else. She once ignored a UTI for so long that the infection spread, and she was hospitalized for days. Rachel nearly killed Mike when he visited Kim in the hospital to ask what he should feed Linnea for dinner. Kim has put everyone's needs before her own for as long as anyone can remember, but Rachel was always the independent one. The corporate badass. She was on top of everything. Type A to a fault. If her check engine light came on, she'd drive directly to the mechanic to get it diagnosed. How in the world did she let these symptoms go on so long without telling anyone? Kim has been replaying every conversation since the day of the diagnosis, trying to remember if Rachel mentioned anything about pain, soreness, or unusual symptoms, but she can't come up with a single memory other than Rachel mentioning a sore back after moving Linny into the dorms. Rachel really kept it inside while the disease spread throughout her organs.

Her friend Sophia, who had a horrible attitude when they were children but has somehow grown to be an incredibly thoughtful woman, excuses herself from Rachel's bedside for some fresh air. When she exits the house through the patio doors, she finds Kim sitting on the back deck, taking a long drag off a cigarette and staring ahead at a yard full of nothing at all.

Sophia pulls up a chair, and Kim offers her a cigarette from her pack. Immediately, Sophia shakes her head before thinking it over and shrugging as she holds her hand out to accept one. She leans forward while Kim flicks her lighter and touches it to the end.

"I haven't smoked one of these since I was eighteen," Sophia says before stumbling into a fit of coughs. Kim can't help but smile.

"It's like riding a bike; you'll be fine. If there was ever a day you need one, it's today."

"She's not going to be with us much longer, is she?" Sophia asks.

Kim begins to shake her head when she's overcome with an urge to sob, which doesn't happen often. She and Rachel are "tough broads," as her dad used to say. Her chest heaves as she fights to keep it in.

"I'm not sure how much longer she has, but I think it would be a good idea to tell her everything you want her to hear before she goes. Don't leave any unfinished business."

Sophia considers this for a minute before pushing the end of the cigarette into Kim's ashtray on the table between them and hopping to her feet.

"Thank you, Kim. We've all wished you were our older sister more than once since we were kids. Rachel is so lucky to have you."

She nods and takes off into the house before Kim can respond, which leaves her sitting on the deck with wetness at the corners of her eyes. Once the patio door closes, Kim finally allows herself to sob, and she doesn't care who hears it. Her sister, her sweet, wonderful sister, is leaving her. "Life can be so fucking cruel," she whispers.

"WERE YOU SMOKING?" Rachel asks as Sophia reenters the room. "Since when do you smoke?"

"First one in over twenty years, and it was just as glorious as I remember. I might even feel high," Sophia responds.

"You can't get high from a cigarette," Monica says as she reaches forward to adjust Rachel's pillows for the fifth time since they arrived.

"Says someone who has never smoked one in her life," Rachel quips.

"I have something to say. Something to confess," Sophia announces, steadying herself for the reaction her words are about to elicit. Rachel sits up a little straighter and motions for her to continue.

"Remember senior year when we were having that sleepover at Jen's and the boys came to toilet paper the house? We ran outside with a carton of eggs and started pelting them before we realized they also brought eggs and we were under attack?"

"Obviously I remember; I ended up in the ER after that eggshell got stuck in my eye. Why are you bringing this up?" Rachel asks.

"It was me. It was me who threw that egg at you. Not the boys."

All three women gasp, and then nearly fall over from the laughter that erupts.

"It isn't funny! I have felt horrible about this for over two decades, and I never told a soul. Not even my husband! It's the worst thing I've ever done."

"I'm sure it wasn't on purpose, Soph," Jen says, wiping her eyes while the other two have yet to contain themselves.

"It was," Sophia responds, barely above a whisper.

Rachel gasps. "Soph— Why would you hit me on purpose?"

"Because you agreed to go to prom with Petey Buckley and you knew I liked him," Sophia says with a shrug, like that's a perfectly sane reason to throw a raw egg full speed at somebody's eye.

"But I refused to go to prom with him because I was convinced he was the one who egged me. I went to the dance by myself and had to wear a pirate patch!"

"Wait, didn't you make out with Petey Buckley that night at Berg's camp after prom?" Monica nearly shouts, pointing at Sophia.

She once again shrugs.

"Well, it all turned out okay in the end now, didn't it?"

This time, she can't help but laugh along with them.

"Any more confessions before I kick the bucket, ladies?" Rachel asks, looking around the room and wiping her face with tissue.

"I lied to you guys about losing my virginity to that guy from Iron Mountain. We only kissed before I panicked and left the movie theater. I was just jealous of you all and didn't want to be the only virgin," Jen says with a shrug.

"Oh my god, I lied about it, too!" Monica says. "I never went all the way with Travis because he had a zit on the end of his nose that was about to pop, and it grossed me out too much."

"You two pathetic virgins," Sophia says, leaning forward to high-five Rachel. "At least Rach and I were cool enough to get laid."

"I don't think anyone has ever described you two as cool." As Mike leans his head in the doorway and delivers his line, the women jump.

"And I don't think anyone has ever described you as anything other than an asshole," Sophia responds.

"I wear it well, though, don't I?" he says, winking at

Rachel before disappearing down the hallway toward the master bedroom.

"I still can't believe your sister ended up with Mike Way. If you would have told me that when we were sixteen, I would have laughed in your face," Monica says.

"Laugh? I would have cried," Rachel responds. "Please don't let him be the last face I see before I die. I don't want to die angry."

"When the end is near, we'll lock him in the basement," Jen offers.

"Nah, let him stay in the garage working on his bike. He won't even realize what's happening until the hearse arrives to take me."

As usual, Rachel means for this to be a joke, but the mention of a hearse quiets the room. No matter how much these women have prepared themselves to lose a friend, none of them are quite ready to say goodbye yet.

From the moment they were old enough to leave the neighborhood on their bikes, Rachel has been their protector. She's been a smart aleck her entire life, and that smart mouth has spewed the most perfectly timed insults at any fool who dared to bother them. They may not talk every day like they used to, but Rachel is always the first name that comes to mind when they need someone they can depend on. None of them are sure what they will do when that person is gone.

For the next hour, they tell stories and reminisce about the old neighborhood, but none of them are really invested in the conversation, as their minds drift to losing Rachel every time it's her turn to talk. They fixate on every word, wondering if it's the last night they'll spend with her.

"You know we love you, right?" Monica asks. "You know you're the greatest friend we could have ever asked for, and we're so lucky to have had you this long?"

Rachel exhales. "I love you guys so much," she says, weakly putting her arms forward as each woman leans in, placing their hands on top.

They cry, quietly at first and then each one louder as they realize this may be the last time the four of them sit around telling stories. Life can be so cruel.

Twenty-Eight

"TUESDAYS WITH AUNT RACH," Linnea attempts to singsong, her voice cracking before she can finish the sentence.

Rachel hasn't left the bed in twenty-four hours, nor has she eaten anything. Everyone knows what's coming, but nobody wants to say it out loud. Thankfully, she's still alert and cognizant enough to carry on a conversation, albeit weakly with slow, sometimes slurred, speech.

Dr. Lam stopped by early this morning on his way to the office and delivered additional pain medication for Kim to administer. "At this point, give her whatever she needs," he instructed. "Let's make her comfortable."

The tear he hastily wiped from his eye as he was leaving confirmed to Kim that it won't be long now, and also that Rachel is more than just a patient to him.

"They gave me the good stuff, kid," Rachel says, turning her head on the pillow to face Linnea, who is now sitting in her favorite chair. "I'm high as a kite."

"That's good, Aunt Rach. That's great," Linnea responds, her voice once again betraying her at the end. She's trying to hold it together, but damn, this is tough.

Kim is at the grocery store buying ingredients for a chili recipe that predates either sister. Their grandmother made it for years before it was passed down among the women in the family. It's late summer, but it's the first thing that came to mind when Rachel considered what one of her final meals would be. She's not sure she can stomach more than a bite or two, but she'd like to die with the world's best chili in her system. Drifting into a permanent sleep with the taste of her grandma's secret seasoning mix on her tongue will make her feel like she's landed in heaven, even if she doesn't earn a spot in line for the real place. She just knows that her sister is sobbing in the aisles of Elmer's County Market as she places the ingredients in her cart.

"I've got another story for you, but it's not going to be easy to hear. Think you can handle it?" Rachel asks, her words slow yet concise. Linnea nods. "And I'm going to close my eyes while I tell you about it because I'm tired. It's a horrible story, but it's important to me that you hear it."

"Of course, Rach. Of course. Relax and take all the time you need," Linnea says, jumping to her feet to close the bedroom door before returning to the reading chair. She knows the drill when Rachel is telling her the stories of violence and revenge. She doesn't need anyone overhearing before she's gone.

"You remember the letter, right?" Rachel says, bending her arm slightly at the elbow and pointing her index finger up toward her pillow. "It's so important that you read it the minute I'm gone."

"Yes, ma'am," Linnea assures her. "It's not blank, is it? You've played so many pranks over the years, it just occurred to me that this could be your final one."

Rachel manages a slight upward twitch of the lips, nearly a smile.

"No such luck, my dear. I'm too tired for pranks."

"Fair enough. So, who is this final story about? Do I get to hear about the demise of another asshole?"

Rachel opens her eyes slightly to look at Linnea before her eyelids become too heavy to lift. She squeezes them tightly closed before continuing.

"I lied to you, Linny. I'm sorry."

"Lied to me? About what?"

"I panicked when you asked me what happened to my fiancé, Lance, after I left him. I told you he died when a propane tank exploded and burned our house down, but that was a lie. He didn't die in a fire."

"Well, how did he die?" Linnea asks, leaning forward.

"He didn't die when I left for that work trip. I came back and listened while he apologized and promised he'd learned his lesson. Against my better judgment, we got back together, and I married him."

Twenty-Nine

I KNOW what you're thinking—how could I have married the man who cheated and lied so many times? Unless you've been in a relationship like the one we had, I'm just not sure I can explain it.

For so long, I told myself, "At least he's not abusive," because I didn't think of what he was doing to me as abuse. Obviously, in the year 2025, I now know it was emotional abuse. Back then, I thought if I didn't have a black eye or broken ribs, I couldn't relate to being a battered wife.

He begged for my forgiveness and promised he'd change, just like cheaters do. That's the worst part—I *knew* to expect him to grovel. Everything he did and said was so predictable. I don't know if I could admit it at the time, but when we had our brief separation, I also found out Eddie had moved on. The man who was always in the back of my mind had found his happily ever after and I felt like I couldn't do any better than Lance if I couldn't have Eddie; that's the life I apparently deserved. I don't think I ever would have gone back to him if Eddie had been available. I would have done whatever I could to have a relationship with him, but I drew the line at contacting him when I knew he was taken. After being the victim of cheating so many times, I didn't have it in my heart to do that to another woman, no matter how strongly I believed he was my soulmate.

About six months after Lance and I were married, he hit me for the first time. He looked as stunned as I felt. I'd never been hit by anyone before, man or woman. I remember it stinging like hell as he dropped to his knees and begged me to forgive him. He explained how hard his day had been at work and how he was exhausted and wasn't thinking straight. I barely registered the words as they came out of his mouth. All I could think was, *He hit me. He actually hit me.*

It's so horrible of me to say now, but I always heard stories of battered wives and looked at them as weak. I wondered why they didn't just walk out the door and leave the bastard. Why didn't they hit back? Call their fathers? Call the police? It took one punch to the face to erase all those silly questions from my head because you'll never understand it until it happens to you.

I was embarrassed. Can you believe that? I was ashamed, and for what? What did I do wrong? He was the coward who hit a woman across the face. A woman he vowed to love and protect until the end of his days. Why in the hell was I the one feeling shame?

It was pretty quiet in the house in the days following, but as any abused woman can tell you—of course it happened again. Any man capable of hitting a woman is bound to do it more than once. It's not something that a decent man accidentally does just once. You either have it in you to abuse a female or you don't.

Sometimes it was a slap across the face, sometimes it was a shove into the wall. Maybe he didn't like the dinner I cooked, so he'd shove the plate in my direction with so much force that steaming sauce would splash all over my face and neck, leaving red marks that lasted for days. Like I told you before, he'd always been a bit of an asshole, but never like this. And I'd always been a strong woman. What had happened to me?

When my mom and dad would plan a visit, Lance wouldn't touch me for days for fear that my dad would see the bruises. I begged for my parents to plan trips more often so I could have a break from the constant abuse.

We were remodeling the bathroom in our house, and Lance was having issues laying the tile. I made the mistake of asking my dad for help while he was in town for a visit. He was able to show Lance how to properly cut the tiles to line up around the toilet and in the corners, which was exactly what he'd been having issues with. He smiled and thanked my dad for his help when they were done; I think they even shared a beer together to celebrate the bathroom being finished after months of it being a construction zone in our house.

I walked my parents out to the car, as I always did, and the minute their car pulled out of the driveway, I heard a loud noise come from inside the house—like some sort of engine or machine. I sprinted inside, and I remember thinking that our furnace must be going out. I know that sounds so silly now, but I just couldn't think of anything else in our house that would make such a loud noise when it malfunctioned.

I ran down the hall to find Lance with a small chainsaw-like tool in his hands, the kind we used to trim branches from the yard. He was destroying our beautiful guest bathroom—the very project we'd spent months working on. He was cutting directly into the freshly painted walls, with drywall pieces flying in every direction. With one swift motion, he destroyed my beautiful bathroom light fixture. There was glass everywhere. I couldn't move; it's like my eyes were seeing the destruction but my mind wouldn't accept that it was actually happening.

I'm sure you can guess by now that my husband wasn't very pleased that I had asked my dad for help. According to him, it made him feel like less of a man, and I'd done it on purpose to embarrass him. I didn't know it at the time, but that would be one of my last visits with Dad, who got sick shortly after. He passed away before I could ever tell him what Lance was doing to me.

After the beating I took that night, I called into work for a week with a horrible stomach flu because I wasn't in any condition to be seen in public. That was the first time I considered that he might actually kill me.

Thirty

THE WORST DAY of my life was on a Friday. Isn't that silly—Friday is supposed to be the start of the best part of the week. Anything is possible on the weekend.

It was the middle of January and Lance and I were going on a snowmobile trip with a few other couples we hung out with. They weren't the same couples that he used to drink in the shop with; we had moved to a new town by then, in an attempt at a fresh start. These friends and their wives weren't overly warm to me, but they were friendly enough. At first, I enjoyed the random dinners or dive-bar nights with them, but it became a chore when I would spend an hour trying to cover my bruises with makeup and then sit across from the wives all night, begging them to notice. I just wanted them to sense that *something* was off so they'd ask some questions and do something to help me. That day never came.

I'm sure you're wondering why I didn't just leave him and go back to my parents' house—sounds easy enough, right? Well, I grew up in a Catholic house in the nineties, and I'm not even sure I can explain Catholic guilt to someone who hasn't experienced it. My father had passed away by this time, and my mother got really involved with the church during her time of grief, in the months before she got sick herself. I loved my mom, but she would have found some way to make the failed marriage my fault. Lance charmed her each time they were together, and I'm not sure she'd even believe me if I told her how bad it was. Nonetheless, I lay in bed at night wondering what would happen if I snuck out and just showed up at her door and asked for my old room back. I can't tell you how many times I stared at the car keys hanging on the wall and felt like I might actually do it.

He also controlled our bank accounts. By that time, I was making just as much money as he was, yet he paid the bills from our account, put me on an allowance, and kept anything that was left over. He spent so much on his stupid Jeep, the money could have allowed me to retire years early instead of going toward a lift kit, engine mods, and a custom paint job. He was living the good life while I was pinching pennies. This is why I was so shocked when he took me shopping for a new snowsuit before our big trip.

We were going to spend three days on the trails up in the national forest, stopping at dive bars along our path and ending each night at a trailside motel. I wasn't much of an outdoors person, but I was just so happy that he wanted to spend all this time with me and even felt I needed a fancy new snowsuit for the occasion.

At this point, I don't think he'd laid a finger on me in weeks, and I foolishly believed maybe he had grown out of it and realized that violence wasn't the answer. We weren't exactly in a blissful state of union; I was still walking on eggshells around him, but I wasn't in physical pain, and that became the closest I could come to bliss.

We pulled into the sporting goods store, and he let me walk through the automatic doors before him; this sticks out in my mind because he never let me go first. He never opened doors for me; he simply stormed in front and let the door close in my face if I wasn't quick enough. Each time he did it, I thought about Eddie. Although I only interacted with him in person when he would deliver to our office, he always opened the door if a female was entering the building at the same time—it's one of the first things I noticed about him. I couldn't imagine how nice it would be to have a man opening doors for me everywhere we went.

Not only did Lance offer to let me pick out a snowsuit, but he also had the patience to let me try on a few sweaters while we were at the store. This was also a rarity. Again, foolish, I know, but I really thought it had finally happened—he was trying to be a better, more patient man. Maybe we could work this out after all. I even imagined growing old with him and joking about the days he used to lose his temper with me, because they were such a distant memory.

By the time I tried on the third sweater, his entire demeanor changed. He wanted to pay for the snowsuit and get on the road, even though we had hours before we were scheduled to leave. I couldn't figure out what had set him off; we were doing just fine.

He sped through the parking lot to his Jeep, and I remember thinking that he must have an upset stomach; that would explain his sudden change in mood and urge to get home quickly. I didn't question him because when I'm not feeling well, the last thing I want is for someone to try talking to me; I just want to get home.

The first time Lance hit me, I never saw it coming, but I learned to expect it going forward. There were telltale signs that he was about to strike. That snowy Friday afternoon, it came out of nowhere. Once we got on the highway, he kept his left hand gripped to the steering wheel and started punching me with his right. He gave me a jab to the eye that I was certain would do permanent damage.

"What? Why? Why are you doing this?" I cried, holding my hands up in defense as I scooted as far away from him as possible. "I thought we were having a good day!"

"Yeah, we were until your fucking boyfriend decided to text you. I just knew you were fucking around," he spat out through gritted teeth before punching me in the ribs.

"What? What boyfriend? What are you talking about?"

He threw my phone at me. I didn't even realize it wasn't in my purse. I hadn't touched it since before we arrived at the store. With shaking hands, I looked at the screen and saw a text from Eddie. There couldn't be worse timing; I hadn't talked to him in years. The most puzzling part of this entire situation is that the text was harmless.

"Hey, friend! Long time, no talk! I just had to let you know that I was watching The Today Show and they were talking about Gladstone, what a small world. Figured I should check in—hope all is well!"

"Lance—he literally says, 'long time, no talk.' How in the world does that equate to me fucking him? Are you serious?"

Lance gave a condescending laugh before pulling off the side of the road. We were on a county road about three miles from the house. It had been snowing all morning, and the temperatures were in the mid-twenties.

"Get out of the Jeep," he said, his voice so even and unemotional it gave me chills.

"What do you mean?" I asked. "We're three miles from home. Just drive home. We can talk about it there."

Without a word, he got out of the Jeep, walked around to my side, and pulled the door open. I was so shocked, I barely registered when he unclipped my seatbelt. With one arm, he yanked me out of the Jeep and threw me to the side of the road. I remember going from praying that nobody would see this because I was embarrassed to praying that someone would drive by and save me.

"You must think I'm a fucking idiot," he said before kicking me in the stomach. He was wearing his work boots. The blow to my gut was worse than any pain I'd felt in my life. For days, I had tried to put it out of my mind that my period was late, but when he kicked me, it's all I could think about. What if there was a life growing in my stomach and he just destroyed it? What if he destroyed a part of me, and I could never have children at all?

He took my purse and emptied it into the snow and then wound his arm back and pitched my phone into the field as far as he could. With several feet of accumulated snow, I knew I'd never find it. Before I could collect my thoughts, he was gone.

I know I laid there for a while, trying to catch the wind he had knocked out of me and tried my best to convince myself there was no way I was pregnant. I just had a late period because of the stress, that's all. I got to my knees and eventually to my feet, gathering whatever personal effects that I could before jamming them back into my purse. I was missing my driver's license and insurance card, but that would have to wait for another day because I was freezing and needed to start the walk home before I froze to death out there.

It took over an hour, but I made it to our neighborhood. When our house came into view, an unfamiliar car was in the driveway. My thoughts raced. Had someone called the police? Did someone witness what he'd done to me? Was this some sort of social worker and was I going to be saved? This may be the moment the nightmare would be over.

I couldn't feel my fingers or my toes by the time I got to the front door. I lacked the control over my body to open the door gracefully. I simply swung it open and saw Lance standing in the kitchen with a woman I'd never seen before. I stumbled in, collapsing in a chair at the breakfast table.

She appeared to be around our age, but you could tell she probably smoked too many cigarettes, drank too much booze, and spent entirely too much time in the sun because her skin was horribly damaged, and her teeth were yellowing. You could have knocked me over with a feather when she reached over and placed her hand over his on the counter.

"Who . . . who are you?" I asked though chattered teeth.

She didn't answer; she just looked at Lance to explain.

"I wanted to tell you sooner, but there just wasn't a good time. This is Shelli. She's going on the trip with me. We'll be back late Sunday night, so I'm sure you can have your shit out by then."

I couldn't form a full sentence in my mind.

He just took me shopping for a new snowsuit, left me for dead on the side of the road, and is now leaving me for this random woman I've never seen before?

The question in my mind should have been *Why is he acting so nonchalant when he almost just killed me and then made me walk three miles in the dead of winter?* Yet, all I could think about was why he would let me pick out that snowsuit. I was so out of my mind, the snowsuit shopping somehow hurt worse than the rest. He was never planning on letting me go on that trip.

Being raised in the Catholic church meant I was taught about forgiveness. I knew all about confessing sins and how

God loved everybody, and you could punch your ticket to heaven if you just said sorry for the things you had done.

That was the moment I decided I would no longer believe in God if he was capable of forgiving Lance for everything he'd done to me.

Thirty-One

LINNEA IS STARING AT RACHEL, who still has her eyes closed tight. Linnea's not sure she's ever felt pain like what she's feeling now; her stomach is twisted in knots and there's an anger brewing inside her that she doesn't recognize. She squeezes her own eyes shut, trying to push down the rage.

"Tell me you killed him. Say it. Tell me it was a slow death. Rachel, just tell me he's gone," Linnea whispers, tears streaming down her face. "Tell me he never hurt anyone ever again."

She opens her eyes to plead with her aunt Rachel for information when she sees wet streaks begin to trail down her cheeks, as well.

"Rachel, tell me you weren't pregnant, and tell me he's dead. That isn't the woman I know—you're not weak. There's no way you just let that bastard get away with almost killing you. I can't believe you let someone do that to you for so long; you've taught me better than that. You've taught me to be strong."

Rachel takes as deep of an inhale as her body will allow and turns her head away from Linnea.

"Linny, I'm so tired. I'm just so tired. Please let me rest for a minute and I'll tell you, I promise. I just want to rest."

Linnea stares at her in disbelief for several moments before realizing that Rachel has drifted off.

How could she leave the story like that? Linnea needs to know how Lance died. Her trembling hands reach up in the direction of the envelopes under Rachel's pillow, but she stops when she thinks better of it. She promised she'd wait until she's gone to read what she has to say. She prays the letter will tell her what she did with Lance's body so she can go spit on his unmarked grave. She's never hated someone so much in her life.

Linnea recalls the evenings spent on the back deck with her mother when she was preparing her for high school. Her mom would often say things like, "Linny, you need to under-stand that not all people are good, and that's a hard pill to swallow." She knows not all people are good. Hell, some of them are malicious, but something about this strange man abusing her aunt makes her want to punch something. Burn down a building. Go to an open field and scream. How could anyone hurt Rachel like that? How did he sleep at night after treating a woman that way? He was a fucking monster.

A few light taps on the bedroom door momentarily snap Linnea out of her rage, and she's able to wipe her tears away before her father completely enters the room. He sucks in a quick breath when he sees Linnea's reddened eyes, and his gaze travels to his sister-in-law, lying unconscious in the bed.

"Is she—"

"Dead? No. She's just resting."

"Oh, thank God." Mike exhales. "I mean, I know it's coming. I'm just not sure if I'm ready for it to be today."

He walks around the bed and puts an arm around Linnea's shoulders.

"Dad, why wouldn't you tell me a story about Aunt Rachel when I asked? You've known her for most of your life. Surely there's some special moment you've shared that you want to tell me about."

When Mike smiles, his eyes crinkle at the edges and it reminds Linnea of how seldom she sees her father wearing a joyful expression. He's always stressed about work or bent over, focusing on some project in the garage. She can't remember the last time he genuinely laughed in her presence, outside of an errant chuckle here and there.

"Well honey, like I told you—she was always your mom's pain-in-the-ass little sister. I didn't spend a whole lot of time with her growing up," he tells her, rubbing his hand on her back, the dry, cracked skin from his palm getting caught on her sweater.

"What about college? Or when you and Mom first got married—you lived in the same town as Aunt Rach, didn't you?"

She really wants to scream, "Why didn't you save her from that monster?"

Mike takes a seat at the foot of the bed and places a hand gently on the comforter, under which Rachel's legs are neatly tucked.

"Yeah, she's always been close to wherever your mom was. I guess I took that for granted. It's going to be strange not having her around. Even if she is a pest," he says, wrinkling his nose. He's talking to Linnea like she's a child, which annoys her endlessly.

"Did you like any of her boyfriends? Did you think she'd marry any of them?" Linnea asks, knowing she's playing with fire. She can't help it; she needs to hear her dad's response.

Mike blows out a ragged breath and shakes his head.

"No, sweetie, I don't suppose I did. She had a knack for

choosing assholes, ever since we were growing up. None of them deserved her."

"Do you love her, Dad?"

Mike's head jerks up to meet Linnea's gaze. "Why would you ask me that?"

"Because she's been your sister-in-law longer than I've been alive and you're about to lose her. I think it would be a wise decision to tell her you love her."

Mike nods, collecting himself before he turns to Rachel, who still appears to be sleeping.

"Rach, if you can hear me, I love you. Of course I love you. You know that . . . Surely, you know that?"

Linnea smiles, satisfied that she could at least get her dad to do the bare minimum.

"Want to go sit on the porch and wait for Mom? It's beautiful out."

"I suppose I could sit for a minute before I get back to work," Mike responds, leaning forward to squeeze Linnea's knee before standing. "Let's go, kiddo. I think your aunt needs some rest."

Linnea observes her father as they leave the room, and the way he looks at Rachel confirms her suspicions. He's destroyed about losing her; he just isn't emotionally ready to admit it. Don't men ever grow out of hiding their emotions?

Thirty-Two

MIKE LASTED all of five minutes "relaxing" outside with Linnea before he made a half-mumbled excuse about having to finish some project in the garage before dark, as if he doesn't have an entire shop filled with expensive overhead lighting specifically for nighttime projects. She's learned to enjoy the five minutes here and there that he's willing to spend with her, rather than being annoyed over the hours he's absent—focusing on the negative will drive her mad.

With Kim still out running her errands, Linnea slips back into Rachel's room to check in on her. She's pleased to see her aunt's chest rising and falling with each breath. She's resting, but she's not gone.

She tiptoes around the room, straightening things up while Rachel sleeps. Growing up, Aunt Rachel's home was always spotless, and Linnea knows it must be driving her crazy to lie in that bed while the rest of the room is cluttered, but she also bitches at Linnea for "fussing" any time she starts to tidy up. Getting it done while she's unconscious is the only option.

Most of the mess is comprised of napkins, tissues, Post-it notes with random, unintelligible scribble on them, empty pill bottles, and boxes from over-the-counter drugs. Matching pairs of earrings are scattered across the tops of each of the dressers, as Rachel quit caring about wearing jewelry weeks ago. She's taught Linnea that accessorizing with jewelry is the perfect way to complete an outfit, but you've "got to keep it understated" and would point to her own as an example. Linnea replayed those words the first time she saw Rachel lying in this bed without any jewelry at all, which was a shock.

Rachel's wallet is lying open on one of the dressers, most likely from the last time she tried to force a few hundred-dollar bills in Kim's hands to repay her for the groceries. Kim continues to remind her that she's not eating enough these days to affect her grocery bill. Linnea pauses when she sees Rachel's library card sticking out from one of the thin card slots.

It's such a silly thing to push her over the edge, but the thought of Rachel never being able to go to the library again knocks the breath right out of her. What if she has books checked out—is Linnea responsible for finding and returning them? Should she stop at the library and inform them of Rachel's death when she's gone? She scans through the rest of the cards in her wallet—health insurance, car insurance, credit cards, several store loyalty cards, and an unused gift card for Bath and Body Works. Linnea is overwhelmed with the thought of handling everything when Rachel is gone. She wants to help her mom, but where to begin? Who do they even call when Rachel stops breathing—911? Do they need to inform social security? It's all too much. She closes the wallet and places it back inside Rachel's designer handbag. A handbag that she guesses will be hers, as her mom refuses to use any accessory that costs more than thirty dollars. "Quit fighting it; luxury feels good," Rachel once told her sister.

"So does being able to feed my family," Kim had replied.

She's startled by a sudden inhale from Rachel, and it reminds Linnea that she's still here. She's not gone yet. She doesn't have to deal with final arrangements today. Rachel is alive, and Linnea can still tell her everything she needs her to hear. It's not too late.

She rushes to her chair, scooting it up against the bed so she can grab Rachel's hand.

"Rach, you know I love you, right? You're the best aunt I could ever dream of. You've been there for me every day of my life and I'll never forget it. You're such a good aunt. You're such a good aunt," Linnea repeats, burying her face in the comforter next to Rachel's body. She's still breathing steadily but appears to be in a deep slumber. Although she doesn't respond, Linnea just knows she can hear the words she's saying. She's still in there.

After composing herself enough to quit sobbing, she places her hands on the mattress to prop herself back up to a sitting position and laughs when her hands brush up against several piles of wadded up tissue tucked underneath the comforter. In the early days, Rachel would ball up a used tissue and toss it across the room, most of the time making it in the small trash can outside the bathroom. The last week or so, she's been too weak to throw anything, so she crumples them up and tucks them under her body. Linnea isn't sure what the end game was here, but she's going to help her by disposing of them all before she wakes.

"This can't be comfortable," Linnea whispers as she feels for more balls of tissue under Rachel's sleeping form. She pulls the trashcan next to her beside the bed and sees that it's nearly half full of used tissue. "You are so nasty," she whispers again with a smile.

Setting the trash can down, she gently places both hands under Rachel's side and lifts slowly to check underneath her and see if she's gotten all the trash. Under her lower back, she sees two more tissues and a nearly empty tube of lip balm. She stops when the sight of a tattoo peeking out from the waistband of her pajama bottoms comes into view. She didn't know Rachel had any tattoos; she always lectured Linnea about them, warning her not to litter her pristine body with words or symbols that might not have any meaning to her as she grows older. "You want to put something permanent on that body of yours? It better be damned important to you because you're going to be staring down at it when you're ninety-five years old. You're going to be very disappointed if it's the name of a boy you thought was special in your twenties, so you paid some back-alley tattoo artist to put his name in cursive next to your hoo-ha."

Although it feels like a violation, her curiosity overpowers any moral dilemma she may face about pulling Rachel's waistband down an inch to see the tattoo.

She inhales sharply.

Then, she reads the names. They are printed in matching black font with a single line drawn through each one.

Tyler.

Brent.

Marcus.

Lance.

Her Aunt Rachel literally drove to a tattoo shop and had the artist permanently add a list of the men she's killed to her ass, complete with a line crossing the names off her list.

Linnea thought nothing else could shock her about Rachel's secret life, but this is something else.

This also confirms for her that Rachel *did* kill Lance, even if she didn't have the energy to finish telling Linnea the story.

Against all odds and every ounce of her body begging her to have a morally decent response, she smiles.

Hell yeah, Aunt Rach. Hell yeah.

Thirty-Three

WHEN HER MOTHER ARRIVES HOME, Linnea helps put away the groceries and straighten up the kitchen before she announces that she's going to go to the library. Seeing Rachel's card made her realize it's been entirely too long since she checked out a good book and sat in front of the expansive windows overlooking the lake to unplug and read for an hour or two. She's wound tightly from staying in the house and knows it would do her good to take a breather and have a change of scenery before her mental health spirals.

"You'll call me if she wakes up?" Linnea asks.

Kim stops chopping onions and places a hand on the counter.

"Linny, sweetheart, she's just resting. You can go do whatever you want, and she'll still be here when you get home. Just be back by supper time, or I fear your father will eat all this chili before you get any. He's asked me when it will be done three times, and that's the most interest he's shown in one of my dinners for at least a decade."

Linnea smiles. She yearns for any sort of normalcy right

now, and her family's famous chili recipe might be the only sense of comfort she's going to have for a while.

"I'll be home for supper; that's a promise. Love you, Mom."

She peeks her head in the garage to say goodbye to her dad on the way out, but he barely looks up from his work bench, instead waving a dismissive hand in the air and shouting, "Alright, sweetie. Have a good day," without questioning where she might be headed.

As she's buckling her seatbelt in the driver's seat of Rachel's Volvo, which she was basically forced to start driving by her aunt, she hears her phone vibrate with a text inside her bag. Pulling it out, she smiles to see it's from William, a guy she's been crushing on from spring semester at school.

She reads his words and for the first time, she notices how dismissive and short he is with her. She's been enamored with him all semester and is so delighted when she receives any communication from him that his tone gets overlooked. Now that she's thinking about it, he isn't very kind at all. Have her Aunt Rachel's stories changed her expectations when it comes to men? Something about the horrible things she's experienced has made Linnea realize she won't be accepting anything less than what she deserves going forward. Nobody's life is perfect, but the least she can do is try her best to learn from her aunt's mistakes so she can have the best chance at happiness.

With a smirk on her face, she leaves him on read and puts the car in reverse. For the rest of her life, she's going to remember the things Rachel has taught her and, assuming she's able to watch over them in the afterlife, Linnea is going to make her proud. Rachel may have only spent forty-one years on this earth, but her life is going to mean something. It's going to have an impact that will last for the rest of Linnea's.

Halfway to the library, she realizes she's been driving in silence, so she turns the radio on and smiles when a local station announces their next throwback jam, "You Oughta Know" by Alanis Morissette. Linnea turns the volume up to max, rolls the windows down, and sings the parts she knows at the top of her lungs. Then, she pulls into the library parking lot and sobs for fifteen minutes before she exhausts herself and gives up.

She's never experienced a loss like the one she's facing, but she's old enough to understand she's going to have plenty of moments like this—uncontrollable grief and helplessness, followed by acceptance and resolve before the cycle repeats. Just because she's aware of the pattern doesn't make it any easier.

After pulling down the visor and flipping open the lighted mirror, Linnea spends a few moments applying just enough makeup to cover her swollen cheeks and puffy undereye area. From her car to the double doors of the library, she encounters two familiar faces but, luckily, they both simply wave hello and keep walking. She's holding herself together, but any questions about Rachel would threaten to unravel her without warning.

Linnea scans the help desk after entering the library and smiles. Her favorite librarian, Jane, is working, so she makes a beeline for the desk and asks her for a recommendation.

"Afternoon, Jane. I'm looking for a book that is so beautiful, it makes me happy to be alive. I need to forget my problems for a little while. Nothing too deep; just a nice, happy book."

"Say no more," Jane replies, leading Linnea over to the

fiction shelves. She scans them with her finger before landing on the S's. "*Saturday Night at the Lakeside Supper Club* by J. Ryan Stradal. This is the one."

With a wink she hands it to Linnea, who accepts the book without hesitation. For the next three hours, she loses track of time and forgets her every worry as she gets lost in the pages of a book that hits so close to home, she's surprised it takes place in Minnesota and not here in northern Michigan. Every emotion, every nuance of having an extended family, the Midwest quirks—he just nails it. She reads until her eyes ache. Linnea can't remember the last time she's felt this lost in a book. This is what a great author can do—make you forget about life for a while. She makes a mental note to send this man an email. She's not sure if he'll respond, but she needs to let him know how one of his books saved her for a few hours during a very dark time in her life. The author's name sounds familiar, but she's not sure if she's read any of his other work, so she reaches for her phone to look it up. She has a gift card leftover from her birthday and thinks that buying his backlog would be the perfect way to spend it.

Her heart stops when she pulls her phone from the bag and sees three missed calls from her mother displayed on the screen.

She silenced her cell out of habit when she walked in the library and got so distracted by the book, she didn't even consider that there could be an emergency. Rachel was sleeping. Her mother assured her it was the perfect time to get out of the house and take a breather for a few hours.

She drops the book on the table next to her, grabs her bag, and hurries out of the library. She'll apologize to Jane later.

"Linny?" her mother answers the phone.

"Mom, I'm so sorry. My ringer was off. What's going on?"

"Linny, baby, you need to come home. Can you come home?"

She doesn't need to ask. She knows exactly why she needs to come home. It takes everything she has not to fall to her knees right there in the library parking lot.

Thirty-Four

"She was awake right after you left for the library; she was feeling so good. She even wanted to help me with the chili. I couldn't believe how good she looked. I almost called you to come back so you could see her like that," Kim says between sobs.

Linnea's arms are tightly wrapped around her mother's body, rubbing her back as she speaks. She always imagined it would be her mother consoling her when this moment finally came, but she has somehow found the strength to be there for the woman who just lost her only sibling, the last remaining member of her immediate family.

"My head is pounding," Mike says, walking through the living room from the garage. "I need to lie down for a minute before all the chaos begins."

"Chaos?" Linnea asks.

"I want you to say your goodbyes to your Aunt Rachel, sweetheart," her mother says. "I'll give you a few minutes, but then I have to call the funeral home. They'll send someone to officially call her time of death, and then they are going to have to take her."

Kim barely makes it through the final words before her shoulders start heaving again. The thought of strangers entering her home and packing Rachel up to take her away is too much to handle. When she considers that Rachel may be all alone tonight in a cold, dark room, she can barely breathe. Linnea can't help but think that it should be her father consoling them both, but he's hiding his head in the sand, as usual. Kim peers over Linnea's shoulder and watches every step Mike takes as he disappears down the hallway. If looks could kill, he'd be dead. *We don't need him*, she thinks. *We can handle this.*

"Mom, I need you to know something," Linnea says, her stomach turning at the thought of these secrets being out in the open.

"Of course, sweetheart," she says, pulling away to look Linnea in the eyes, but not letting go of her hands. "What is it?"

"Rachel kept saying that you don't know anything about the things she did, but you've been together your entire lives. I know there's no way you're completely in the dark."

"The things she did? What do you mean?" Kim asks, her eyes growing wide with concern.

"I need you to know she told me everything. Tyler, Brent, Marcus, Lance—I know it all. And I still love her. I love her so much, Mom."

Now it's Linnea's turn to erupt in sobs as she holds her mother tight. As they pull away, she hesitantly looks in Kim's eyes and is met with a look of confusion.

"She told you about the Majestic Gents?"

"What the hell is that?"

"Tyler, Brent, Marcus, and Lance. They were members of this band she used to be obsessed with in college, the Majestic Gents. She went to every one of their shows. Hell, she even got their names tattooed on her butt and paid me not to tell Mom and Dad. She couldn't afford to get it removed when the band broke up, so she had some hack job tattoo artist she was dating draw black lines through each of the names. It looks ridiculous. What in the world did she tell you about them? They broke up a decade ago. I think they're all accountants or something now."

That doesn't make any sense.

There is no situation in which the four men Rachel offed happen to have the same names as the members of her favorite band. That would be impossible.

"I'd like to say goodbye to her alone, if that's okay," Linnea says in a hushed tone, ignoring her mother's questions about the names.

Although her brows are still furrowed in confusion, she nods and looks toward Rachel's closed bedroom door.

After a few deep breaths, Linnea walks to Rachel's door like a zombie. She's devastated, she's tired, and nothing is making sense. She slips inside the room, closing the door behind her.

She's not sure what she expected Rachel to look like after being dead less than an hour, but it's so much better than any version of her dead body that had been running through Linnea's mind on the drive over. She's heard the words, "she just looks like she's sleeping" so many times in books and movies, but it's the truth. Her head is hung a little unnaturally to the side, but she otherwise looks exactly the same as when Linnea left her to go to the library.

After a brief hesitation, she even leans forward to check for a pulse. Finding no heartbeat and a hand that feels a little cooler than it should, she accepts that Rachel has passed. She no longer feels the need to hold it together in her presence.

She holds Rachel's limp hand and cries for the loss of her

favorite aunt, and just when she thinks she's finished crying, she begins again when she remembers her friends, her coworkers, all the people who loved her. Linnea and Kim will need to call everyone to let them know what happened. Linnea can't imagine how many times she's going to have to say the words out loud. *Rachel's gone.* She thinks of the line of people who will be at the funeral, and then she wonders what they will think when they find out Rachel was a murderer. Linnea made her mind up that she won't be delivering the Michigan State Police letter until after the funeral is over. Her family deserves the right to grieve before Rachel's reputation is tarnished. She'll tell the cops she simply didn't find the letter until they began cleaning out her room after the services.

Wait, the names. The names of the murder victims. Did she lie to Linnea so she wouldn't search online for details surrounding the deaths? She's been so busy with school and being grief-stricken over the impending loss of her aunt, the thought never crossed her mind to search online for more information about the victims. Did she think Linnea would track down the unsolved cases and turn her in? The thought makes her stomach turn. She'd never do that to Rachel.

Linnea stares down and her hands, both now wrapped around one of Rachel's. She strokes the top of her aunt's hand before flipping it over to inspect her palm. She remembers the so-called world-renowned psychic they encountered on a trip to Wisconsin Dells a few years back. She took one look at Rachel's palm and told her she had one of the longest life lines she'd ever seen. "See, Linny? This nice lady says I'm going to outlive you both." The woman smiled and nodded in agreement. What a con artist.

Linnea gently sets Rachel's hand back down on the bed beside her.

With shaking hands, she reaches under the mattress and pulls out two envelopes.

The contents of these envelopes have been on her mind since that fateful day months ago when Rachel first told her of their existence.

Flipping them both over in her hand, she stares at the handwriting on the outside.

After a short deliberation, she starts with the thickest one.

It's labeled FOR LINNEA.

Thirty-Five

My Sweet Linny,

As these letters always begin in the movies, if you're reading this, it means I'm gone. I hope you are handling it as best you can. In moments of sorrow, please remember this: You were the best niece I could have ever dreamed of. I knew the moment you were born that there was something special about you, and not just in the way that every aunt feels about her firstborn niece. I knew you were going to be someone who changes lives. You changed mine when I realized that being childless didn't mean I wasn't capable of loving someone more than life itself; I learned that kind of love exists the moment I saw you, even though you were naked and screaming.

Never for a second doubt this: I know how much you love me. There is not a doubt in my mind. Those quiet, sleepless nights where you stare at the ceiling and wonder if you told me enough—rest assured that you have. I have felt nothing but love from you and your mother every day we've been together.

If all goes as planned, I have told you all the stories of the horrible things I've done in my life. I also hope by the end of those stories, you have grown to understand why I did the things I did. You understand that these men were horrible, evil beings who aren't capable of change. In order to ensure that you'd understand these complicated situations, I had to fib a little.

Tyler, Brent, Marcus, and Lance don't exist. Well, they do, but they were actually in this band that I used to be obsessed with, and they were four names I knew I could keep straight when I was telling you those lies.

The biggest lie I've told you is that most of these things happened to me. They didn't. Although I knew all the words by heart, they weren't my stories.

If you're wondering why I've followed your mother everywhere, from college, to Lansing, and back to the U.P., it's because I couldn't leave her. Especially after our parents died. If I had any balls, I would have done more, but the best way I could think of protecting her was to stay close and make myself always seen. To let it be known that wherever Kim was, I was there watching.

Linnea, I know these words are going to be so hard for you to hear, so I need you to take a deep breath before you read the next line.

Did you? Deep, I mean it.

The names may have been fabricated, but the stories I told you were true, and in actual events, the man was your father.

Your father did those things to your mother.

I am so sorry that you are having to hear this from me now, but I made a promise to Kim a long time ago that I wouldn't speak ill of him in front of you. I don't know why she continues to protect a man who has caused her so much pain and heartache, but I'll never break a promise to my sister. Her desire to raise you in a household with both a mother and a father apparently outweighed her common sense. I've told her a million times that she should take you and run. She has come close on several occasions but just wouldn't pull the trigger. It's so easy from the outside looking in to say, "Why doesn't she just leave? It's so easy," but the truth is it's *not* easy. We will never understand because we aren't in her position. I pray you never find yourself in a similar situation and hope that I've taught you better by now to not even entertain a man who is capable of such cruelty.

Do you know what my mother, your grandmother's, dying words were? "I can't believe he didn't kill him." She was talking about my grandpa. She couldn't believe he let your dad live, and that was before the worst abuse had even happened.

I'm certain the most traumatizing part of my confessions to you was when "Lance" threw me out of his vehicle and kicked me in the stomach before leaving me in that ditch.

It really was a cold, January day when that happened. Once your father left for the snowmobile trip with his mistress (he came crawling back to your mother weeks later after getting bored with her), she called me. She was so scared to tell me that she might be pregnant.

She refused to go to the hospital and instead sent me to the pharmacy for some painkillers and a pregnancy test.

She *was* pregnant.

You were the baby.

I've laid out a lot of plans for my final weeks, and I'm really banking on those plans working out, or this letter will be for nothing.

Linny, when I die, I'll only be confessing to one crime,

and that will be first-degree premeditated murder in the death of your father. My confession to the Michigan State Police should answer any questions you or they may have.

I know you may not understand, but I pray in time that you will.

I love you, please forgive me. I had to give your mother a better life, if it was the last thing I did with mine.

Love, Aunt Rach

PS: Eddie is a real person and he's the man your mother should have ended up with. He loved her more than anything in this world. I looked him up online and he's now a divorced father of two and lives an hour away. The sticky note on the back of this page has his most recent contact information. When your mom is done grieving, do her a favor and contact him. She deserves happiness.

Thirty-Six

L INNY TEARS OPEN the envelope labeled M ICHIGAN S TATE P OLICE, hoping she can foil whatever plan Rachel set in motion. She hasn't begun to let her words sink in and refuses to believe her father is capable of any of the things she's accusing him of. She'll deal with those emotions later.

T O W HOM I T M AY C ONCERN:

I F YOU'RE READING THIS, I hope it means I have succumbed to my terminal cancer. My name is Rachel Lynn Marless, and I killed my brother-in-law, Michael Way.

If you look at my phone's history, you'll see that I began searching for methods to kill him months ago, immediately after my diagnosis. I also have a video in the photo album on my phone where I detail my plans, so you know I was of sound mind when I made the decision. That sorry excuse for a man has terrorized my sister for over twenty years, and it will be my great pleasure to be the reason he can't hurt anyone again.

My plan is to grind up enough of my painkillers and mix them in one of his meals. From what I've read online, I need to make it a meal that is spicy or flavorful enough to overpower any taste the medication may have. My early thoughts are to use my family's chili recipe (award-winning, by the way), but that may change as we get closer. I've found several sites online that allowed me to calculate how much I'd need to kill a two-hundred-pound man, and I've decided to add a little extra for good measure.

My sister and my niece, Kim Way and Linnea Way, have absolutely no knowledge of my plans. They are not involved in any way. I am acting alone. They are good women, and if they knew my intentions, they would undoubtedly stop me from carrying through with the plan.

This is going to be a hard task to complete as I'm dying, so I'm really hoping the powers that be will bless me with this "terminal lucidity" that I keep reading about. That last push of energy before I kick the bucket. I've already crushed the pills and I'm keeping them in a plastic baggie in my nightstand, tucked inside a bag of the gummies I've been taking to sleep at night. If Mike Way is still living when someone reads this letter, please dispose of the white powder you find. My plan did not come to fruition.

Mike is a narcissistic abuser who has committed more atrocities in this lifetime than you could imagine. I understand you'll have to print my name in the news when this all unfolds, but please do me the final favor of mentioning my abuse allegations against him. I don't want this town thinking I took a man's life for no reason. He is the scum of the earth and deserves a much worse death than the one I'm granting him.

. . .

THANK you from beyond the grave,
    Rachel Marless

PS: If you try to involve my sister or niece in this investigation or anyone in your precinct questions their innocence, I will haunt every last one of you until your dying day.

"Mom!" Linnea yells, jumping to her feet. "Mom, where's Dad?"

She bolts out of the room and turns right, remembering his plans to lie down for a nap. Running down the hall, her socks slide on the hardwood floors when she stops at her parents' room. The door is wide open, and she finds her mother sitting at the foot of the bed. She's staring at Mike, who is lying in the same position as Rachel—on his back, hands at his side, chest completely still.

Kim can't bear to turn her head and face her daughter.

Linnea drops to her knees, but she can't manage to make a sound.

Rachel.

She did it.

Rachel killed her father.

Thirty-Seven

ONE WEEK LATER

"SHOULD we feel bad about not following her wishes? I mean, she put it in her will."

"Linny, I don't care what she put in her will, we are not playing 'Look What You Made Me Do' at her funeral. We're just not."

Linnea smirks at the thought of Rachel's lawyer typing that in the legal document, just doing what her client is paying her to do. The guests will begin arriving shortly, so a man from the funeral home is pulling down the projector screen to start playing the slideshow they've prepared of Rachel's life. Both women exhale when "In My Life" by the Beatles begins to play. They both can agree it's a much better choice, despite Rachel's request.

Kim wraps her arm around Linnea's shoulders as they stand alone in the viewing room. Their eyes aren't on the casket, but instead on the loop of photos projected on the screen of Rachel's life. Forty-one years condensed into a four-minute slideshow.

So much has happened in a week, but the most important conversation came when Linnea confronted her mother about her father's behavior. She didn't get into details; she simply asked a series of questions.

"Mom, was he abusive?"

Kim nodded.

"Did he hurt you when you were pregnant?"

Another nod.

"Did he ever hurt me?"

Kim's head snapped toward Linnea's direction. "No, Linnea. Never. I'd never let that happen."

"Mom, was he a horrible person?"

Kim considered the question for a minute before hanging her head and giving one last nod. The women didn't speak of it again. Someday, Linnea might ask more questions, but for now she has all the answers she needs.

Mike will be cremated after the investigation into his death concludes, which the lead investigator has promised Kim will not be long. It's a fairly open and shut case with a full confession video and letter; they don't have much else to investigate. Call it a small-town miracle, but they've also agreed to keep his manner of death and the confession by Rachel private until after her funeral.

The women don't plan to have a funeral for Mike.

As the slideshow concludes with photos from Linnea's high school graduation and starts over again with Rachel's baby pictures, the owner of the funeral home approaches Kim and Linnea.

"Are you ready to receive guests? There's quite a line outside."

"Ready as we'll ever be," Kim responds, and both women move to the right of the casket to greet mourners as they arrive.

For the next two hours, they receive condolences from hundreds of attendees. People came from miles away to pay their respects to their former student, coworker, lover, and friend.

Both Kim and Linnea break down several times when people from Rachel's past show up to tell them how much they loved her. By the end, it becomes a blur of names and faces they won't remember encountering tomorrow.

Once the visitation is over, everyone moves across the street to the church basement, where a reception is held with drinks and snacks. Linnea isn't sure she can handle any more hugs and squeezes, and Kim has nearly lost her voice from all the expressions of gratitude she's given this afternoon. They are both looking forward to an informal gathering rather than a receiving line so they can have a break.

In the church basement, Linnea makes a beeline for the serving plate overflowing with Scotcharoos and several carafes of hot coffee. It's now nearly four in the afternoon, and she can't recall eating anything since she woke up. She always tries to start her mornings with a positive thought about the endless possibilities of how great the day can be, but this morning she was simply smacked in the face with the realization that today was the day they'd be burying her favorite person on earth.

She finds an empty table without anybody who is going to hug her neck while they sob, and then she collapses into a metal folding chair before eating her dessert in two bites. She'd kill for a glass of wine and a two-hour nap right about now.

After going back to the snack table to grab a Rice Krispies Treat and a scoop of Jello, she's met by the gaze of an older woman with kind eyes and a Jackie-O hairstyle.

"You must be Linnea," the woman says. "My name is

Marilou Thomas, and I had both your mother and your aunt Rachel as students when I taught high school English."

"Mrs. Thomas, it's a pleasure to meet you. Thank you for coming. I've got to know how my aunt Rachel was as a student," Linnea says, shaking the woman's hand while balancing a plate with the other.

"Well, Rachel had a tough start to high school with everything that happened, but by sophomore year she seemed to have a clear head and a steady resolve to be on the honor roll. She was a pleasure to have in class; always so organized yet creative."

"A tough start?" Linnea asks with a slightly cocked head.

"I'm sorry, dear. I figured it was something your aunt or your mother told you about. There was a horrible accident the summer before she started high school and her boyfriend was killed. It was such a tragedy. You know how young love is; your aunt was absolutely devastated after he died."

Linnea's head is spinning. There's no way.

"How, um, how did he die? If you don't mind me asking."

"Oh, it was horrible. He and Rachel apparently had a little lover's quarrel and he thought he'd drink his sorrows away down at the park. Kids that age shouldn't be drinking at all, and they sure as heck don't know how to handle their liquor. He had too much and fell off something and hit his head. I can't remember if it was the top of the slide or the playhouse, but he died on impact. I'll never forget that summer; not just because of the death of Jackson Northcutt, but because we had a once-in-a-lifetime tornado a few weeks later. Anyway, once Rachel got some therapy and began to heal, she really was the best student. She was always so kind and happy, like she'd never suffered a tragedy at all. There are certain kids that teachers never forget, and she was one of them. Very special. Anyway, I'm so sorry for your loss."

Linnea doesn't move when the woman walks away. She can't wrap her mind around what she just heard. In Rachel's confession letter to Linnea, she said the stories were about her father. That she'd made up the names to cover for the fact that they were all Mike. Did she really kill her boyfriend the summer before high school started?

She doesn't have much time to overthink the situation because she's quickly consumed by a group hug from Rachel's three childhood best friends. Jen, Sophia, and Monica sob while they recount stories that Linnea has already heard countless times. She doesn't interrupt them; she simply listens to the tales and wonders if any of these women knew what Rachel did that fateful summer. She so badly wants to ask about Jackson Northcutt—Tyler in Rachel's story—but she can't find the words. Before she can consider how to bring it up, the women have moved on to the refreshments.

"Linny, I have someone I want you to meet," Kim says, motioning toward a beautiful woman with dark, raven hair and olive skin. She appears to be around Rachel's age.

"Wow, I haven't seen you since you were a toddler. What a beautiful woman you've grown to be. I'm Rainey. I was your aunt's roommate all four years of college at CMU."

"Rainey?" Linnea asks, willing her pulse to slow down. Rainey exists. Of course she does; Rachel's stories were littered with half-truths.

Kim is pulled away by a group of older women from the church, leaving Linnea and Rainey alone.

"Rainey, Rachel talked about you. You were her favorite person in college. It sounds like you guys had some wild times," Linnea says, unable to find the words to verify Rachel's account of watching Rainey's boyfriend die on the floor of their dorm room. There isn't a tactful way to ever bring something like that up, but especially not at a funeral.

A wide smile spreads across Rainey's face.

"Your aunt was the very best. We had so many good times together. Honestly, they were the best years of my life."

Before Linnea can ask another question, they are approached by another unfamiliar woman. Rainey leaps to her feet and throws her arms around the woman's neck.

"April! I haven't seen you since college," Rainey cries.

Before the woman can respond, her jaw begins to twitch, and she takes a deep breath. It takes about ten seconds for the twitching to stop, and the woman laughs.

"It's gotten a lot better since our Central days, eh?"

Rainey doesn't respond, she simply leans forward and squeezes both of the woman's hands and smiles. "It's so good to see you."

Linnea can't stand it anymore. She's tired, she's emotional, and she needs answers.

"I know this is going to sound crazy, but my aunt told me stories about you both before she died, and I just need to know if they were true or if she was losing her mind because of the disease."

They both turn to Linnea, confusion on their faces.

She continues. "Rainey, did you have a boyfriend freshman year who died of alcohol poisoning?"

Linnea can't believe her boldness; she barely recognizes herself. Desperate times call for desperate measures, and she needs to know if Rachel's stories were true or if they really were versions of things her father had done.

"I did, Linnea. He wasn't a great guy, but it was such a sad situation. Your aunt is the one who found him unresponsive in our dorm."

She can't dwell on the details. She turns her attention to April. "And April, did my aunt have an altercation with a guy who was rude to you at your graduation rehearsal?"

April's shoulders don't sink from embarrassment; she no longer allows that emotion in her life. She does, however, recoil slightly as she recalls the vulgar words that idiot spewed from the row behind her.

"She did. I asked her not to, but that's how Rachel was when it came to protecting her friends. She'd stop at nothing to make sure we were okay."

Next, Linnea asks what happened to that guy, but she knows the answer before April even finishes telling her about the tragic turn his life took that weekend on the Chippewa River.

ONE WEEK EARLIER

As she lies on her back, head propped up by two of Kim's overpriced goose down pillows, she wills herself to sit up by pushing off the mattress with her elbows and leaning her head forward. She's been listening to the sounds coming from the kitchen for over an hour, and she knows the chili prep is complete and it's now simmering on the stove. Mike is in the garage, and Kim just closed the bathroom door down the hall, so she only has minutes.

She's heard the expression, "it took every ounce of energy I had" but never lived it until this moment. Every fiber of her being was begging her to lie still and let death take her, but she had made a promise a long time ago that killing him would be the last thing she ever did in this life. With all the effort in her tiny body, Rachel pushes herself to a sitting position and slowly swings her feet to the floor.

"You can do this," she whispers.

With trembling legs, she manages to stand and, one step at a time, makes her way to the door. She nearly falls before steadying herself by grabbing the door frame. Her hands never leave the smooth, cream-colored walls as she makes her way to the kitchen, the plastic bag of crushed pills crinkling in the pocket of her pajama pants each time she takes a step.

She abandons the safety of the hallway walls for the three or four steps it takes to make it to the stove, and it nearly derails the entire mission when she trips forward and falls into the back of one of the dining table chairs. The sound is just loud enough to be heard beyond the kitchen, so she stops momentarily to make sure she doesn't detect Mike or Kim heading her way. After a few seconds of silence, interspersed with the sound of a power tool grinding in Mike's garage, she stumbles a few more steps and ends with one hand slapped on each side of the stove, bracing herself on the counter.

Rachel breathes a sigh of relief when she sees four bowls stacked neatly to her left, so she won't have to reach up into the cabinets to retrieve one. Then, her heart drops when she remembers the fourth bowl is for Linnea, who could be home at any minute.

It's now or never.

Reaching into her pocket, she wraps her skinny fingers around the plastic bag and pulls. Although it weighs next to nothing, she has a hard time gripping the top of the bag with the throbbing aches that are shooting through her wrist and knuckles. She didn't take any medication this morning so she could be as clearheaded as possible for her final mission, and the pain is beginning to border on unbearable.

"Damn it," she whispers when the bag falls to the ground. Luckily, it's still sealed tightly, but she's overwhelmed thinking of the strength it will require to bend over and retrieve it from the kitchen floor.

Holding onto the counter with one hand, she begins to

lower her body before losing balance and crashing into the cabinets beside her. She nearly jumps out of her skin when Kim appears next to her on the ground without a word, scooping up the bag of powder with one hand that is tucked into her long shirt sleeve and wrapping her other around Rachel's miniscule forearm to steady her. Rachel didn't even hear the toilet flush, let alone detect her sister's footsteps down the hall.

When they are both back to standing positions and facing each other with the pot of chili and plastic bag between them, Rachel speaks. Her voice is low and hoarse, but she manages to get the words out.

"He came into my room last week while you were gone. He told me he couldn't wait for me to die because I'm the last person alive who could tell Linny everything. You . . . You have to let me do this, Kim. It's for you. Everything is for you and Linny."

Kim shakes her head as a single tear rolls down her pale cheek.

"Please," Rachel says, barely above a whisper. "Please let me do this. It's taken everything I have to coexist with him in this house and pretend for Linny's sake that I don't hate her father. Now I have to leave . . . I can't leave you two alone with him."

Again, Kim shakes her head and leans past Rachel to grab a bowl from the top of the stack. She pours a ladle of chili into the bowl and then looks at her sister.

"The whole bag?" Kim asks, without emotion. "Or do I need to measure?"

Rachel's eyes grow wide. Her head is nodding before her brain acknowledges what is happening. "The whole bag," she whispers.

Kim once again wraps the end of her sleeve around her

hand before grabbing the bag and empties the crushed pills into the bowl, pours a second ladle from the pot, and grabs a large spoon from the drawer next to her. She doesn't look at Rachel while she stirs, mixing the liquid so thoroughly that the powder essentially disappears. There isn't a moment of hesitation in her movements.

"No fingerprints," Kim whispers and tucks the bag into Rachel's front pocket.

She sets the bowl on the counter, leads Rachel back to her room with a steady, supporting grip, and tucks her in, just as she does every night.

Kim leans over, kisses Rachel on the forehead, and whispers, "I love you more than you'll ever know. You've been the greatest sister, and I'm so sorry I never had the courage to leave. I hope I'm showing enough courage now for you to forgive me."

"You've done nothing to need forgiveness for. You thought staying was the right choice and I can't pretend to know what it feels like to be in your position."

Rachel's breaths are becoming more rapid before she manages one long exhale and continues.

"Kim, I need you to know I told Linny some of the things Mike did to you. I didn't tell her all of them, just enough for her to understand. I told her they happened to me; that I was abused by my ex-husband, named Lance. I just needed her to understand how bad it was. I needed her to know what it feels like to hear about someone doing those things to someone she loves. When she finds out it was you, she'll understand."

"Ex-husband?" Kim asks and Rachel manages a shrug. She's never been in a relationship that lasted longer than six months or so. Her sister always came first and that was too much for most men to handle. "Did you tell her about the day of the snowmobile trip?"

Rachel nods. Her eyes are beginning to feel heavy.

"I love you, Rachel. You deserved a better life than one spent looking out for me."

Kim doesn't say another word before slowly standing straight and turning on her heels to leave the room. Rachel can't help but notice that she purposely leaves the door cracked open just enough. She wipes a tear while she listens for what's next. She's so tired, she's not sure she can stay awake to find out.

The only sounds she hears are footsteps as her sister walks down the hall and through the kitchen, opens the door to the garage, and yells, "Mike, your chili is ready. Get in here before it gets cold."

"Coming," he yells in response.

Rachel feels the weight of the world lifted from her chest and, within minutes, she falls into a deep, eternal slumber.

* * *

The Award-Winning Marless Family Chili Recipe

1 tablespoon of any damn oil you want to use

1 small yellow onion, diced

1 jalapeno, minced – leave the seeds if you're brave enough

1 clove of garlic, minced *updated 2003 – okay to use jarred

1 pound of ground beef – NOT lean, this is not a diet meal

1 can of chili beans, do not drain

1 large can of diced tomatoes, do not drain

2 tablespoons of chili powder

1 dash cinnamon, 1 dash brown sugar

Salt and pepper to taste

Heat the oil in a large pot or Dutch oven. If you are living on your own, you should have a dutch oven. You should own this before you purchase a microwave. Then add the onion, cooking until softened.

Add the minced jalapeño and sauté for 2-3 minutes. Grandma Marless says use wooden spoon.

Add garlic and sauté for another minute.

Add the ground beef to the pan and cook until it's brown. Use common sense. Drain if too much grease. Don't pour down the drain.

Add the beans and tomatoes, including the juices, to the pot.

Add chili powder, cinnamon, brown sugar, and salt and pepper. Stir to combine.

Simmer on low for one hour.

Serve with saltine crackers. *updated 1999 – Fritos are also good

Acknowledgments

I remember after I published my first book, Underground, my better half Cash said, "One day, we'll be celebrating your tenth book!" That number seemed unreachable, and here we are – book number TEN!

I'm never comfortable with listing the names of those who helped with the process because I'm always so worried that I'll forget someone. I'm going to name a few who helped shape this book, but please know there are dozens more who probably should be listed and accidentally omitting those names is what keeps me up at night.

First, for my friends and family who lent their names for characters in this book. Let me remind you: Just because I named a character in your honor, it does not mean the character is BASED on you. So please don't call me with complaints about how your character behaved, hah! And for the friends and family who lent me their stories of mistreatment, frustration, and abuse: thank you for allowing me to tell your tales of survival and perseverance. It's the first time I've ever had to stand up from my laptop while writing because I felt I was going to be sick.

Dr. Dave and Lindsey, thank you for always answering my medical questions and never inquiring about why I'm asking such strange things.

To The Escanaba Public Library (especially Jane), thank you for being a wonderful (and mostly quiet) place for me to write this book. The closest I've ever come to a fist fight was defending a librarian from being disrespected by an unruly patron and my only regret is not actually punching him. Surely someone would have paid my bail in the name of protecting our libraries.

For Carly and Erika, thank you for being the best editors a girl can ask for. I always write the acknowledgment section *after* the book is edited, so any mistakes are proudly my own. I sprinkle commas in like they're going out of style, I know.

Brandon, brainstorming with you to come up with cover designs is more fun than it should be. You are so talented and I'm forever grateful for you.

For my best friends, thank you for always sticking with me even when I'm a hermit because I'm writing, having a panic attack because I need to face the public, or going into a momentary depression because I'm convinced everyone is going to hate whichever book I'm writing. You guys handle those mood swings without flinching and I don't know what I'd do without you.

To my ARC readers, there is a reason I haven't launched a full advanced reader distribution program and it's because I already have a group who I can trust to have my work in their hands early. I never worry that one of you will share my book to a pirated site, post spoilers online, or commit any other atrocities. I can't tell you how much I appreciate you always having my back and also my best interests in mind.

Finally, to you, the reader: I don't think you understand how grateful I am for this life you allow me to continue living. Whether it's posting a review, recommending my book on social media, or just telling a friend – you are the sole reason I'm able to continue doing this for a living and I will never, ever take it for granted.

If you'd like to reach out, I try to answer every message I receive as soon as I can.

Email: info@jlhyde.com
FB: Author JL Hyde
TikTok: AuthorJLHyde
Instagram: BookAndBeerReview

9 798987 163160